The Ranas of Solan

Dr S.C. Narula completed his undergraduate studies in Physics and Astronomy, followed by a post-graduate degree in English Literature. He went on to earn his PhD from Delhi University. His doctoral dissertation focused on Milton and was subsequently published as the *Milton Handbook: A Study of the Poetry in the Office of the Pulpit & the Ludlow Masque and Some Shorter Poems*. The chapters comprising this work originated as presentations at academic conferences and Milton Seminars, garnering him global recognition.

Having travelled extensively, he has contributed numerous research articles to distinguished international literary journals. His initial venture beyond academia was The Third Passenger, a collection of poems published in 2016, which has now entered its second printing. In the same year, he published his second compilation of poetry, titled *Inheritors of Broken Sky*. Furthermore, he has penned several volumes of short stories and a novella titled Damyanti: Woman of Substance.

Dr Narula has earned acclaim for his skill in translating Urdu, Punjabi and Hindi poetry into English, a role he undertook for the esteemed Sahitya Akademi (India's National Academy of Letters) and Rupa Publications. He has also been honoured with the Dhaka Translation Fest (2018) Lifetime Literary Award.

The Ranas of Solan

SUBHASH CHANDRA NARULA

RUPA

Published by
Rupa Publications India Pvt. Ltd 2023
7/16, Ansari Road, Daryaganj
New Delhi 110002

Sales centres:
Bengaluru Chennai
Hyderabad Jaipur Kathmandu
Kolkata Mumbai Prayagraj

This is a work of fiction. Names, characters, places and incidents are either the product of the author's imagination or are used fictitiously and any resemblance to any actual person, living or dead, events or locales is entirely coincidental.

P-ISBN: 978-93-5702-595-9
E-ISBN: 978-93-5702-596-6

First impression 2023

10 9 8 7 6 5 4 3 2 1

Printed in India

To Manu

1

To fix the period of the events enumerated, it should suffice to say that it was 1945–1946 when India was closing in on the fructification of the surging Freedom Movement against the British Raj. It culminated in the final, strong and serious statement at the Quit India Movement, spearheaded by loin-cloth sporting and a long-staff wielding Gandhi—the Mahatma, as Tagore called him—whose presence, or even the mention of his name, sent cold shivers down the spine of the rulers of the day. Winston Churchill thought that Gandhi was endowed with some occult magical powers that bewitched the diplomat and the envoy sent by the Crown to control the mounting strength of the Freedom Movement led by Gandhi and invariably turned the tables on them. Churchill resolved never to meet Gandhi face to face.

Intelligent and no less shrewd than the imperious and expansionist British, Vikramjit Rana had started to get a new abode built for his family, away from what he knew was going to be the lot of Jinnah's Pakistan. And he had been and would be in Gujarat, near Sialkot (now in Pakistan), where he was a sub-divisional magistrate since the previous six years.

Now, it was time for him, by Machiavellian strategies, to burrow into the inner coterie of the rulers. And he was amply rewarded in exchange for his loyalty and compliance to the limit of identifying himself with the rulers' intentions. Remaining in the good books of his superiors, promotions came easily, and his position in society and his lifestyle climbed several notches rapidly. Papered with the acquired gold foil of sophisticated tastes is the tendency to metamorphose into depravity, to show the elemental foible; and man, therefore, in pursuit of his desire, can lose awareness of when he begins to cross the line without a qualm or contrition.

The family estate of the Ranas was, in fact, a whole hillock, four to five hundred feet above road level, on the southern side of the Kalka–Simla Road. Simla, by its location at around seven thousand feet above sea level in the lower Himalayan range, with its weather, was not only the summer capital of British India but also a popular hill station for the rich and prosperous. It boasted of facilities such as an ice-skating rink, skiing slopes at Kufri and Narkanda and a nine-hole golf course a few miles beyond Simla. His estate was in this midway town of Solan, between Kalka and Simla, just short of where the shops began appearing in the market area on both sides of the road. And here, too, on the northern side of the highway, on relatively level ground, was the bus stand. The Khalsa Hotel was also located there, the wayside eatery opening to the road, popular amongst the passengers and locals for delectable dishes. It remained busy with crowds going in and out of the small, muggy, cramped hall where the fare was served. It was always filled with thick or thin cooking fumes that could cross-surfeit the flavour of the frying aloo paratha at the entry—an all-time staple and favourite.

The bus stop and the shopping area caused a messy bottleneck for the up-and-down traffic on the road. From the metalled road up to the Rana House, on top of the knoll, there was a walking track that went around the grassy slope, with some well-maintained rows of flowers; the grassy slope was sprinkled with some stray wildflowers in pink, yellow and purple hues.

On top of the hillock was the main family mansion, fashioned like a British manor house; and close by, in the neighbourhood, maybe at a distance of fifty yards, was a smaller annexe comprising living quarters—a double-storeyed, well-appointed structure meant to house the honoured guests of Vikramjit Rana.

Both buildings were joined by a narrow path, along the slope of which ran a wooden railing, like the one by the climb from the main road to the house on top; there was a brief turn around the hill that half hid the annexe from the view of the main mansion, and towards the end of it was placed a metallic bench, painted green.

The estate also had a circular wooden rain shelter structured on a reinforced concrete foundation, with two steps to climb, on the other side of the mansion, and the conical roof and seating bench ran around well within the extended eaves. It was a convenient niche to take a breather during warm summer days or to sit sunning on a late winter morning, all wrapped up in heavy woollens, when it got flooded with the morning sun.

His loyalty to the powers that be of the British Raj in India had earned him a cosy corner in the kind estate of the rulers, especially when the general atmosphere was charged with the determined agitations of the people in the streets, in towns and cities, pushing for the final assault, shaking off of the yoke of slavery. Smugly, Vikramjit was gladdened by the rewards and gifts of land he had received from those British hands. Some of the assorted measures were considerately on the part of the powers that be, around Sonepat, in the neighbourhood of the villages Bandepur and Baiyanpur. These villages and more—about forty miles away in Panipat, his native place where his ancestors hailed from—he gratefully accepted. The family already owned some two hundred bighas of arable land.

The land in Solan was of Vikramjit's own choice, chiefly because of the good weather the hill town had year-round, except during mid-December to the middle of February when Solan (not far from Simla, as the crow flies) too witnessed a few days of snowfall. He had visited it during his years of service on the bench of the district courts. And, fascinated by the general atmosphere of the town, enhanced by the presence of the smartly turned-out cadres of the small army unit in shops and public places stationed on the leeward side of the Solan Hill, he had planned to settle down after his retirement. He was charmed by the withdrawn peace of the town. There were lots of pine trees, interspersed with some cedars, on the slopes of the higher mountains surrounding it.

Therefore, without any loss of time, he got the construction of the residence on the acquired land started. He hoped that it might be ready by the time he decided to apply for voluntary retirement from the crown's service and pursue an independent career in law. The awe of his magisterial baton wielded authority enough in this distant town to get him quality building materials from the local market. Also, adequate arrangements were made to employ the workforce, including the services of a shrewd designer-cum-architect, and a troupe of wage earners with an influential local contractor. The workers were meticulous and honest because they had been told who they were working for was the sarkar, the British government itself.

◆

Before it formally entered the proper Solan town, the highway was at a place called Dohrideewar, or two-fold wall. Dohrideewar was a stone structure of two stone walls, likely to be parapet supports of the sloping end of Solan Hill, one coming down along the highway and the other from around the hillside limit of the town to join a corner of the road. Here, the road widened into a sort of a plaza, which allowed two other branching lanes straight into the town and, further on, to Simla. Along the edges, small fruit vendors, a few with wheelbarrows, came to settle, mostly opening their wooden and cardboard cases of peaches, plums, green gauges, apples and figs. One of the turnings led to Saproon, a small suburb of Solan; the other was a sort of bypass, running almost parallel to the main highway, a crude track along the hillside meeting close to the railway level crossing line from Kalka to Simla. It was in the process of being levelled and laid with asphalt to make it convenient, especially for trucks full of the local produce of potatoes and apples, besides other green vegetables. It was to serve as a regular bypass to reduce the traffic on the main road, lined with shops and shoppers crisscrossing the road, adding to the chaotic confusion and close encounters.

At the beginning of the bifurcation, a row of new shops had come up as the sharp slope flattened. One dealing in building materials and hardware was well-stocked, furnished, gleaming and squeaking new. Everything inside revealed that the owners, Hiralal Sood and Sons, were flourishing merchants. It reminded you of the most popular general store: Sood ABC Store, which had two side openings; one opened on the main road for those looking for drugstore and cosmetics, and the other was within the huge open quadrangle of the bus stop, offering a coffee and soft drinks counter and an ice cream counter. The heavily stacked semi-darkness inside held other grocery items. The amplitude of the stockade spoke for itself; the legend declared, 'Buy Anything: Chocolates to Fashion Wear'. Like the other well-to-do elite of the town, Vikram Rana, too, instantly took to be among the patrons of the ABC General Store. In fact, he found the proprietor, Rahul Sood, a knowledgeable man and pleasant to talk to. He was quickly on friendly terms with him, as friendly as a law officer could be with a shop owner. But Rahul deferentially offered to make home delivery of the daily requirements of breakfast things: milk, tea, coffee, marmalade and Kraft cheese, brown bread and muesli and won over Mr Rana's heart.

Hiralal Sood was a shrewd businessman and able banner bearer of the Sood community of merchants and traders. Since he knew he had the means and manpower, he set his sights on the diversification and expansion of his business. His elder sister, Tara's son, had got a diploma in architecture and draughtsmanship from the Department of Science and Technology. He was self-employed, working from home and had managed to get some odd jobs. Durgadas walked up to the construction site. He met the contractor, was introduced to the architect and wangled some odd jobs for himself. A small room on the rooftop, a *barsati*, had been given to him. It was always in a mess, littered with rolls of drawing paper and bottles of chemicals used for preparing blueprints. There was a broad table with a huge drawing board and some papers pinned to it, several pencils—all sharpened differently with their thin and thick leads—and erasers, one of the earlier generation of calculators, second-hand slide rules and set-squares, activated solar batteries, protectors and the rest of paraphernalia were all there. Only Durgadas knew how to get what he wanted. And being observant, Hiralal knew by now that his nephew Durgadas was not only hard-working but also God-fearing and an honest young man who could be trusted. He washed his own clothing and wore a clean shirt every day, caring little about his appearance, unlike other haute couture-conscious young men of his age. He let the first growth on his face grow, leaving creeper-like curls along his jawline and dimpled chin.

Hiralal was going to please his sister to no end and would also give his nephew a permanent business address of his own. Above all, he would not allow any more customers to go elsewhere seeking a good and qualified architect. He created a small office—a really good, well-appointed office—for Durgadas.

To be self-sufficient in almost all aspects of construction, Hiralal already spoke to one of the three well-known building contractors. Rambabu Gupta, who had a husky squeak due to a childhood injury to his vocal cords, was at the top of his contact list, and he had given him jobs good enough for the huge gang of fifty wage-earners under his employ. Now, Hiralal gave him a corner in his spacious shop, a corner for a table and chair, and got him a telephone extension as a concession from the local telephone department. Therefore, his establishment was self-contained, able to meet any demand related to construction in and around Solan. His foresight and planning brought prosperity to him and all the functioning subsidiaries he had surrounded himself with.

2

Vidya, wife of Vikramjit Rana, was essentially a village lass from the vicinity of Sonepat. Of course, her father, Nemchand Sharma, and his family were one of Sonepat's prosperous and well-known families. For his vocational acumen and quiet and sobering wisdom, Nemchand was always counted among the eminent few of the town. During festival times or other public events, family gatherings or marriages, the ladies of the family were always seen decked in heavy gold ornaments and were the cynosure of the coveting eyes of the neighbourhood. Vidya had gone to the local DAV Girls School, a few streets away, close to the post office. She studied up to matriculation there and passed out, obtaining a first division, more than 60 per cent. She was placed among the first five of the best students in the school. She received an award of honour, a proficiency prize, on the annual day celebration of the school and a special mention to sign her name in the golden-edged book, the school's roll of honour.

The prize comprised a voucher for fifteen rupees with which she could get books worth that value. The diligent student that she was, she bought a dictionary and a book on ancient Indian history. She had always been fascinated by the stories and legends from the past, especially the saga of the Magadha kingdom. Chanakya had helped place the Mauryan Chandragupta on the Magadha throne, a welcome change for the people of the area terrorized by the cruel rule of Ghananand, the descendant of Jarasandha, notorious for his heavy indiscriminate taxes and for lynching and bleeding the poor and innocent. The Chambers Twentieth Century Dictionary can still be found on some shelves of the Sharma household, gathering dust. She was very fond of her purchase, and the pages were well-thumbed and browned, with smudges here and there, signs that she assiduously consulted the reference book.

She also went for the concise version of E.J. Rapson's *The Cambridge History of India.* She had to shell out ten rupees from her pocket to purchase this book. Published in England, it cost her more than she had thought it would. But keen as she was to go deep into the history of the times, she bought the book even though it cut into her month's pocket money. And she was immersed in it more single-mindedly than one would be in a detective novel.

She sailed smoothly across the Rubicon of the Punjab University Matriculation examinations and was placed in the first division, having scored 72 per cent marks.

Her friend Radha, two grades senior to her, had fared

even better, with 76 per cent—in the 'Highly Commendable' category, and had gone on to join the local Sanatan Dharam Degree College but had physics, chemistry and biology as her chosen subjects. She secretly cherished the ambition of becoming a doctor. Radha was iconic. She excelled in sports as well. When in her tenth grade, she had participated in two events, exclusive for girls, at the Annual School Athletics Meet, the hundred-yards dash and the four-hundred-yard low hurdles. She had topped and won the first prize in both events.

Vidya and Radha were great friends. They came from similar rustic social backgrounds. What held the people from top to bottom rung together was an ancient moral fabric; at the head of the loom was an attitude of respect for women, veneration towards seniors, and a universally considerate, humane attitude towards one and all in the give and take of life. Propriety and humility, and not egotism or arrogance, was the outstanding attribute that guided familial and social interaction in the smoothly run society. In general, people imbibed and lived by the wisdom of the dictum, 'A healthy mind in a healthy body'. Their smooth and glowing skin shone with healthy fairness, and they were amply splashed with pink, shapely mouths and cheeks, not decked or highlighted by any rouge or lipstick. The country's air, homegrown food and milk cared for their general health and longevity.

Unlike the city's sophisticated girls, the girls of the countryside became liberated young ladies in the corridors of colleges, hostel dormitories and university classrooms. They did not need to wear deodorants or perfumes even though they carried the whiff of the bovine miasma that pervaded and emanated from the cattle sheds. Every morning, they hurried to help their parents at home and went into the cowsheds to milk the cows or the buffaloes, not without squirting a few jets of milk from the teats straight into their mouths—amused and laughing when their faces were sprayed with warm milk from the udders.

In a way, they were more liberated and open-minded than the city girls, who are made conscious of societal morality and have to don the veil of constrained prudery. Whereas the country children, including the girls, had witnessed and personally engaged in the process of calving. They had seen the mother cows lick, cleaning the remains of the placenta, as the newborn moved straight from the womb onto Mother Earth, flailing its tiny straitened legs; they mentally unravelled early on the whole mystery surrounding the stork sailing down from the heaven, bearing in its long and strong beak the basket with a baby. They were also witnessing the mating of cattle in open lots, maybe with mixed curiosity and the blush of discomfiture.

Even with boys of the same age, the ones who went to school or worked in the fields with their fathers and uncles, the girls felt quite on equal and familiar terms. They talked or dealt with them without much inhibition; all communication almost always took place in the presence of parents, aunts and uncles. From childhood, growing up in the villages, everyone knew everyone else, like members of an extended family, and they breathed in a candid openness and uninhibited ambience, ever minding their own business without messing with others' affairs.

The girls felt liberated enough to pull the spindly or elephantine leg of the neighbourhood boys whenever they found an occasion for it. Especially during All Fools' Day or sports days around the festival of Holi, they all joined in the frolic of rainbow hues (chiefly the rose-red gulal that they smeared on one another's faces till it was impossible to recognize each other).

There were other games involving running races and climbing trees. And other jokes, lampooning a teacher from classrooms, stories they narrated and collectively enjoyed, clapping with guffaws. At times, they even sat down in a circular formation and, by drawing lots, took turns in singing or mono-acting a scene from the epic *Ramayana* or the *Mahabharata* or other folk legends of *Mirza Sahiban* or *Heer Ranjha*. Of course, all understood; it was in the context of the festive spirit.

Though there was general song and dance and a lot of drum beating, there hardly ever was a case of transgression of decency or offence made outside the accepted limits of the social matrix.

Indeed, there were freak cases of intrigues where mutual consent was understood to evolve from physical proximity, which led to frequent surreptitious meetings between couples. Familiarity and natural preference led to the intensity of fondness and preference and culminated in a bond of love, and it was no surprise.

The conditioned formation and tempering of the individual, and thus the social character, at the most impressionable time—one's nascence—builds a firm protective armour, which is not easily permeable or affected when subjected to torque.

The presence of Tagore and Gandhi, therefore, was reflected in society's pervasive and accepted values. Transient as they may be, there was the amalgam of interacting cultural influences when freedom allowed. Only dictatorial or recognized Unitarian forces could make sharp alterations to this, which could only end in creating societies of human robots who would live in comfortable, even luxurious, boredom. Of course, steady and stealthy inroads were made by Western lifestyles' imperceptible but compulsive cultural penetration, aped without understanding the spirit or philosophy underlying the surface.

Such intermingling can cause harm rather than good. The resultant cultural state would be but an amalgam of nameless promiscuity.

3

Vidya, too, like Radha, had begun to weave a web of dreams of what she wanted to do with her future; and, therefore, gave long and proper thought to the subjects she must study after matriculation. She had always felt her heart welling up with sympathy whenever she saw or heard of anyone in pain or suffering; in her imagination, she shot forth to be at the side of the one in ague or injured in a road accident and lying drenched in blood. Hopping from one choice to another, she came to a rather abrupt stop when an image swam onto the screen of her mind. She had read the very inspiring story of Florence Nightingale in war-torn Sevastopol, the 'lady with the lamp', in her sixth-class English textbook. Soon, she was turning the idea of pursuing the vocation of a nursing sister in her mind rather seriously. Gradually then, dwelling on the topic, she felt the tempo of her enthusiasm reach a pitch in a few days, and she finally decided upon her choice.

Next, she felt the need to talk about her plans with her father. It would have to be said the next time she got the opportunity to sit with him face to face in his room. He would then have time enough to single-mindedly listen to her and give his consent, with a word of encouragement and assurance to boost her morale to go ahead and brave the challenges, both in the fields of study and in a life lived in devotion to her adopted duties.

The day after happened to be Tuesday.

Nemchand returned home slightly early, and the bold red smear of the tika between his brows writ large on his mien that he had not forgotten to go to the Hanuman temple on his way back home. And not wanting to be disturbed as he gave himself up to relaxed leisure in his easy chair, he took off his turban, placed it on a side table and reclined. Pappu, the cook cum odd-job man, grew busy in the kitchen to get his master's evening tea ready. It was a brew of pure milk, boiled with good quality Brooke Bond tea for long enough on the stove to turn it into a not-very-dark but rich brown brew, strongly sugared, served with a wedge of the best available ghevar from Nathu Halwai, known for the best assortment of confections.

Vidya came in quietly without any vexing obtrusion when she thought her father was through his repast. And indeed, he had just washed down the last bite of ghevar and was in the process of wiping his moustache. He was twirling it after he had laid aside the folded serviette, the hair touched with a strand or two of grey, when she tapped the door, letting him know that she wanted to come and be with him.

Seeing her favourite child, her father gave her a broad

smile and said, 'Come in, my darling girl. It seems from your unusual sober carriage that you have something on your mind you wish to share with your father. Come, sit down and tell me. And you don't need to demur with building up a kind of foundation; you know your father well.'

'It may be serious for me. I see it as a once-in-a-lifetime decision for me. I've been thinking about what to do after the matriculation results. I pondered over the different vocational studies available as a choice for me. At long last, I have come to the conclusion that the best course for me, to suit my temperament, would be to pursue the vocation of a nursing sister, for which I may have to leave my home and stay in a hostel in Delhi, and yes, Delhi is the closest place where this facility is available at Lady Hardinge Women's Vocational Institute.'

Her mouth was dry, having rushed to the end of what she wanted to unburden off her chest. Her voice was choked with tension, and it had to be. Her face was white, and she was faintly tremulous. She looked up at her father's smiling face and, in a moment, shifted to snuggle with him closely—a sob or two venting the last remainders of peaking emotion.

'Come on now, there, there; we have a courageous girl. O, I'm proud of you. Whatever you have told me about what you wanted to do, and how you said it, is nothing if not truly admirable. But from what is in the air, I sense and hear sounds, ominous to me, that bear a message of separation, too, but not the kind you have been talking about. Like you came to see me, I suggest you go and see your Bua—I mean my sister Shanti—and then Sushila, your mother.'

Close by, on the outskirts of the congested, striated small town of Sonepat, was the residence of the Sharmas, a sprawling bungalow popularly called Peeli Kothi, or the 'sunehri haveli' with its facade and outer walls all painted a deep golden yellow colour. It could be spotted from quite a distance and was in the neighbourhood of the newly come-up swanky district courts. The town had shown signs of its growing prosperity in expansive new constructions of commercial and residential places, some even across the main G.T. Road, planned by building contractors, arriving like little colonies. The builders sensed the demand for residential apartments from the gradual extension of small industries from Delhi in the south and Panipat on the other side. It was one of those quiet, peaceful areas dotted with only the small but beautifully landscaped and properly maintained bungalows of the rich and elite of the town, comprising government officials and business executives of new business houses and senior police personnel.

That particular morning, closing in on the warm midday sun full of apprehensions from what her father said to her, Vidya was left with no options but to wait for the right moment to go and see her Bua.

Come Sunday; Vidya knew that her Bua, after a hair wash with her favourite herbal compound of Shikakai shells and a spoonful of linseed oil boiled in a vessel of water and a spoonful of coconut oil, always had a charpoy laid for her in the shade of the rear wall of their haveli. She faced a rear lawn and lovely umbrageous evergreens lining the edge, past which ran the dry ditch. Shanti, who had all the time to herself, lay drying her, now more than half grey, luxurious wavy locks, with a catnap if she liked. Vidya timed it, so she walked around to where her Bua was reclining on fluffy pillows, wholly given to the luxurious warmth. After her sumptuous breakfast, her eyelids drooped, and the morning vernacular newspaper lay aside; she'd had a cursory look at the headlines. A casual look at the cover page showed a picture of Mahatma Gandhi in his knee-length white loin cloth with his long staff in hand. The legend read of his hard-nosed bargaining, reminding the British of the conditions under which Indian troops fought, side by side, with the armed forces of the Allied countries in World War II, thanks to Governor General Lord Linlithgow.

The sensitive senses of Shanti Bua still picked up the approaching footsteps and was a bit startled, for everyone in the household knew that she didn't like her solitude to be disturbed. And bowing to her authority in the family, no one ever dared transgress. From her half-opened eyes, she saw her dearly loved niece, Vidya, demurely walking towards her charpoy. With the support of her pillows, she rose to a semi-sitting posture, her chin and cheek resting on her left hand to face Vidya.

'Good. Vidya, come over and sit with me awhile. I have wanted to have a word with you for the last few days, since last Tuesday to be exact. We have had "happy tidings" from the house of the Ranas of Bandepur in the neighbouring village, about five kos away. I'm sure you know about the village and have heard of the family. They are one of the eminent families of the area and are distantly connected with us, though the kind of connection it once was is lost in hazy antiquity. Land running into hundreds of acres, loaded with richly yielding crops, an extension of mangroves and grafted orange orchards, spreads out far beyond their village—it is all theirs. On this, scores of peasant families from smaller hamlets subsist and thrive. And the eldest son of Mr Kesar Prasad Rana, young Vikramjit, handsome with greyish blue eyes, has recently returned from England. He is now a sub-divisional magistrate in West Punjab. He was sent to England for higher studies in law, and he passed out from the Middle Temple of Lincoln's Inn as a barrister. Even the British respect his profound knowledge and understanding of the law. He was given the appointment of a sub-divisional magistrate soon after his return from England. But it was away from his home in Gujarat, a town in western Punjab—not the sandy province on the southern border of Rajasthan, renowned for their great warriors, like Maharana Pratap who single-handedly protected his kingdom of Mewar in the famous battle against the mighty force of the great Mogul Akbar in the wide valley of Haldighati. Now, in search of a bride for the young man, they have found it fitting to their fastidious standards of status to approach us.'

Gujarat was not very far from Lyallpur, the location of one of the best agricultural universities in the country, and deservedly so because even the British rulers found Punjab to be the largest bread basket of India. It was close to the Punjab–Sind border and equally close to the city of Sialkot, among the first sports goods industry centres. These cities, even today, will be called industrial centres or towns. But the societies still flourish in and breathe the air of deeply formed traditional, cultural and social values in their diurnal business of living. In terms of the pace of life and their lifestyle—they prefer quiet and are leisurely, like a deep-breathing river that has reached the steady course of the plains descending from its rough mountainous terrain. And the river seasonally renews itself and has not yet succumbed to pollution of all the muck of the filthy and congested, ultramodern, mechanized, skyward reaching (not spiritually, however) towards covetously ambitious cities of commerce and industry. And, according to *Srimad Bhagavatam* of Veda Vyasa, we are not yet far gone into the era of the reign of Kali, the god of all that is elementally sleazy, corrupt and outright fraudulent hypocrisy, yet.

The pervasive and unquestioned social order framework affirmed the acceptance of all citizenry. Law and order, though materially incognito, was yet unassailably in place, like the air they breathed, and it gave its stamp to time. These, and such other places, were pockets that remained uncontaminated and flourished beyond the frightfully advancing shadow of what is called sophistication and its consequent depravity, gradually leading to the dropping bar on moral virtues. Today's inferior and stunted Diogenes clan of questioning freaks of every little possible fault line they see, who ferret it out of the fabric, where they imagine they see it, and create a big furore over the warped half-truths of their discovery. There's an established school of deployers of such limiting logic. They fool themselves and their followers with the blinkered view of their discovery. And they, the scornful cynics, go on to build upon such foundations, their rationale of thought to probe the dimension of the mystery of the human condition, their society and the cosmos. The tools might as well be an abysmal mismatch for the stupendous task.

Such prophets exist everywhere and have existed in all times of human history. Indeed, the flip side of their endeavours does give life its lively and kicking attribute, adding spice to a bland, insipid platter of habit. Therefore, does it not make life a challenge at every step to bring out the best in man? And, aren't human beings always a worthy unit of society at any stage of development?

When she spoke to her niece that afternoon, Vidya's Bua was the voice of her contemporaneous society, its matrix deeply embedded to be the lifelong strength of all her judgement and action. The society at large, too, was held together by the traditionally accepted values into which the likes of Vidya were born and reared. It was life akin to that in villages and small towns, of simple slow-paced life, not yet overshadowed by advancing, aggressive, fissiparous, extraneous cultural influences.

This is from where they drew their rock-steady moral strength.

The metamorphosis that emerged from these terrible shadows is of the perspective with man at the centre, and where divinity—the holy trinity embodied in the church—is only for landmark events, such as births, deaths and marriages. The quiet denial of divinity runs through creation. It leaves man grappling with the reality of broken homes to deconstruct and understand it. In the process, he forgets to look in wonder at the heavens, full of those clusters of stars, all in strict order.

Such values that ensue from the standpoint of a brand of sceptical, agnostic materialisms had not yet substantially affected any aspect of life, save the surfaces, mostly in the aping of the glorified Western ways. Money, human ego and the Turk of a cold and megalomaniac selfish interest hadn't yet caught on to obviate all native values. The rising dark billow of a character, taking shape deep in the heaving ocean of time, that but appears as a ripple on the surface, was still shaping up. Elemental tendencies grow and gain strength when the twines of values are snapped or loosened by repeated wanton transgressions. But they take a long while—years, aeons maybe—to soak and permeate to the lowest rungs of society, to impart to the whole era with a stamp of character. As in passing, the present time, according to scripture, has been referred to as the era of Kali, manifesting in the growth and dominance of the grossest human elemental attributes over others, such as the power of pelf and libido with its seat in the human ego.

Likewise, for the convenience of human reckoning, the ancient sages polarised into four segments the unified whole that was considered the entity of time, in abstraction, in its inexorable flux of the cycle of days and nights. That is, the three others besides the present Kali Yuga, which are the Satya Yuga, Treta Yuga and Dvapara Yuga. The generation of sages that came, following in the footsteps of Sankhya, categorized these segments of time. They created each appropriate nomenclature derived from the dominant elemental attribute of the population in each period. Like the spreading shadow of a cloud takes in its ambit, umbra and penumbra, the areas it crosses, the natural elements in the flux of time, too, take in their native attributes to the multitudes by which the period gets its characteristic name. In the course of metamorphosis, it goes through a period of transition, the penumbra, whereby the next element gradually replaces the dominant elemental attribute of its character. And for the period of transition, the amalgamation of the two attributes merge and remain nebulous. The process is slow and takes time. In human terms of reckoning, it runs into an astronomical number of years and aeons. Things remain undefined during the earlier years of transition. Slowly but definitely, the umbra of the core elemental attribute follows, enveloping the multitudes, giving it character and a name to be called by.

Satoguna dominated, and the dominance of Rajoguna succeeded Satya Yuga. And because this Rajoguna is an elemental state that is just about the best—a balance between the chaste Satoguna and the vicious Tamoguna, and between virtue and base vice—is made possible by the added effort of human will. Volitional effort on the part of man alone can help it attain a semblance of balance. This state, therefore, lasts much longer than the others, just like the middle class of a society is the largest. And so, this era is further segmented into two. And the two intervening periods are the Treta Yuga and the Dvapara Yuga, before the onset of the last, Kali Yuga.

The termination of the Treta Yuga and Dvapara Yuga

culminated in two great wars[1], and the decimation of the population brought about by divine intervention: the incarnate divinity of Ram for the first, and the incarnate divinity of Krishna in the case of the Dvapara Yuga. This cycle at the end of Kali Yuga repeats itself interminably. This is man's best-recorded understanding of celestial flux, of which we, on this globe, are but an infinitesimal part.

In bigger cities and their satellites, some stray symptoms of these infernal fires have begun to blink and claim their arrival. The civic guardians and the police force are duly warned and alerted. The change, the curiosity of the new that deserves a trial as it may, in the long run, be disastrous, is natural. Being elemental is unstoppable, like the billow surfacing the ocean in its own timely swell.

---

[1]The first was during the Treta Yuga, celebrated in the epic Ramayana by Valmiki, and the second was at the conclusion of the Dvapara Yuga, celebrated in the epic *Mahabharata* by Vyasa.

4

Suave and with the timbre of native authority, Shanti Bua spoke to her beloved niece. She had decided that Vidya should be made adequately aware of at least the skeletal family history of the Ranas because, after all, she—but for a chance of her refusal—in all probability, was going to be a part of the family. Her parents were already in agreement to accept the proposal that the Bandepur messenger had brought. Of course, it was a big jolt to the private dreams of Vidya.

Tagore has rightly averred that there is nothing to match the endurance in a woman and, if it may be added, equally admirable is the quiet gritty strength of adjusting even in the face of adverse changes of circumstance in life. It is not, therefore, wrongly said that there is always a true woman, true as sap runs, to make a man successful. She always has a deeper perception of the potential and ambitions of the man. Her sacrifices can go striding across rough terrain to glorious conclusions.

Since an impressionable age, Vidya had imbibed the tenacity of ancestral values in the process of growing up in that ancestral haveli. Of course, she was not immune to immediate worldly influences, like all curious, energetic young. She, too, had rolled up her sleeves to brave the challenges of creating a break into life. She, like her friend Radha, had begun to nurture a dream of her own design until came this ominous knock on the door of her private gossamer castle.

In spite of her Bua's guarded broaching of the subject, preventing any shock, and her affectionate tone, Vidya seemed to have braced herself to face the worst.

But what Bua was revealing was meant to be news of joy. In the very beginning, she gave it the epithet of 'happy tidings' from the house of Ranas. And indeed, to the parents and well-wishers, what could be happier than the final settling of a match and the marriage of the marriageable daughter? Especially so if the prospective bridegroom were almost made-to-order, with nothing left to be desired, with his handsome deportment and top-notch social status.

And the match appeared to be settled when the proposal was given tacit approval by the elders. The parental home and its courtyards, the grounds of her romping and rope-skipping, her ripening from childhood into girlhood and finishing school were never to remain her permanent home. Her husband's home and the adoption of her husband's name would always be her permanent identity and address. All done in favour of adding a strand of strength to the idea of family and society.

It is, therefore, an occasion for jubilation as well as a time to shed tears of separation. The incision shall only be seen in scars of healing, which time shall never be able to mend seamlessly. Sundered lives shall thrive like a transplant on separate soils. Breezes alone shall stir them with tear-dimmed memories of uneven brick-laid streets and friends, picnics and little tiffs and jealousies—the second severing of another umbilical cord.

The first severance is of supreme significance, perhaps more so, symbolically, to decide upon the ultimate solitariness of an individual in the midst of populous and bustling multitudes that people the surface of this globe. However, much conditioning occurs while rearing, and many a weak or strong relationship is formed in the journey to the ripeness of puberty. The bearing down of aloneness, by its sudden wayward grip in the middle of day or night's work, speaks of its omnipresence. Man, in whatever circumstance he may be, must be prepared to face the situation by what he has made of himself, aside from the extended helping hand there may be, which must be gratefully accepted, but cannot ever be taken for granted.

The second severance is a necessity for the social fabric to which one belongs. Obligatory for the perpetuation of values, of institutions that hold society in place, in spite of variant freak of some local action (which, by consequence, puts things in perspective, but by its very character, does not affect the scheme of things, the basic structure).

Vidya's Bua, among the elders of the family, with more than sixty-five years of experience, her life has gone through a hundred variations of happenings, had her voice steady and not without unction. So, she continued speaking with her beloved niece.

'I'm sure you have academic ambitions like your other class fellows, particularly Radha, who is away from home pursuing higher studies in medicine. And, to my mind, intellectually, you would easily compare favourably with her. And I believe whatever field of study you choose for a higher degree, that is, if you do, you would fare excellently. But this opportunity has come your way instead. Only the very lucky do not have to sweat and strive to get such an attractive chance, a chance of a lifetime. I would consider it to be no less than wanton to not reach for it, and take it gratefully as God's gracious gift. Sooner or later, there are moments, even in the life of the most successful woman, who has devoted all her competent energy to a cause or an idea or ideal close to her heart and has reached the peak of success, when she is stung by the natural desire of having children and a home that she would shape and preside over. To be a mother is a natural instinct a woman is born with, and any attempt to smother it is going against the indomitable force of the elements of nature. And civilized societies worldwide are structured around nature's innate creative energy, which manifests in replication and foliation of variety in procreation.

'No, no, such a long-winded discourse was never my intention. Perhaps it all comes to you like some remote memory reawakened as I speak about some of these abstract things. They don't surprise you; you seem to understand and imbibe the ideas easily. Trying to put it into words for you may have taken away the subtle truth at the core of what is already there in your mind. So, it all boils down to the fact that not all aspirations of our age of innocence, even though arduously pursued, must always come true. Though it hurts, the abrupt change in direction has to be said yes to, not by sulking but by smiling. It wouldn't take long for a brave and intelligent girl like you to adapt. The taste of the pudding is waiting to be experienced; and sooner or later, all girls, willingly or unwillingly, go through it. The opportune moment must not be allowed to slip by. And this is not a warning, my darling girl, for indeed, warnings are not the best teaching aid, especially for intelligent people like you.'

Vidya, who had been in her quiet attentiveness listening to her Bua and had been following her observations on the message they had received from the Ranas of Bandepur, did not miss the nuances of what her Bua had to say, notwithstanding the philosophical implications of the long-winded and rambling observation-cum-advisory to her niece.

She had done her best to avoid giving a shock to her niece.

After a while, she said (her diffidence was evident to her Bua), 'You know, Bua, nobody could have been as succinct and diplomatic as you. You have made the things pertaining to a girl settling down in life with marriage *vis-a-vis* other choices in several other fields so clear and convincing to me that the choices for my discretion have shrunk to just the inevitable one, which is fulfilling my obligation to my family and society. Life, as ordained, has to be lived to the best of one's endowments, which have a marvellous pliability to evolve and regulate the enterprise despite the abrupt change in circumstances. It seems to me that a person's character and temperament come readymade at birth for the kind of vicissitudes life shall deliver. And sometimes, it appears that all is pre-ordained by the power of a creator, and no amount of willingness of an individual can cause deviation of the course from the given blueprint as its backdrop.

'Now, look at that, Bua, don't I need to be pulled up by you for being an intruder into the world of prolix argument and philosophy, which is your domain by any consideration?

'Albeit, just bear with me, for it seems to me I must let off some steam. Now, look at the queer irony of what has happened. I went to my father's room last evening to tell him about my desire and ambition to do a course to serve as a nursing sister. I wished to follow Florence Nightingale's footsteps in some hospital after my matriculation. And here I am, mentally almost prepared to let it all pass, like the flitting past of a scene from a train window. And though Father wanted me to go see Mother after I've met you, I do not think I'd like a mother to go through this turmoil of emotions if she, too, is going to talk to me about the proposal from the house of Ranas. O, I can't take the sobs and tears of my dear mother for such a cause. I've heard you and understood all implications in the context of my life and society and the family yet to be.

'You can reassure my mother and your brother; they may put the weight off their chest and, joined by you, go ahead and do everything according to tradition and their best judgement. I shall be happy to go along with whatever their decision is. After all, you all love me and are my well-wishers.

'But now, I shall need some time to myself to straighten out all that was in my mind of a different character and bring it all to acceptance. For all this, I am indeed much beholden to the shaping of my mind under your rearing, Bua, and my parents that the trend of the currents of my strong mind remains firmly anchored in the right direction.'

Bua was glad to hear Vidya's views on the subject. 'Your mother is in the kitchen supervising Champa's clumsiness while preparing lunch.' Tempting smells come wafting from the kitchen and tell of a delicious Sunday lunch for the family. 'We'll meet them at the table, but let me whet my appetite with a short snooze if I can,' Bua said and straightened herself in her most comfortable posture on the charpoy.

Solan

5

Vidya straightaway went into her room to recline in her easy chair, laid with a couple of cushions, but not with the book that she had been reading—Swift's *Gulliver's Travels*—which was left upside down at the page where she was. She snuggled into her brown study and remained immersed in a world of conglomerate memories, and here the strands of desire and aspiration formed a rounded reality of the present. Despite her monition of having to leave her tenderly created world, her innate strength to sail across stray turbulence already did half the job. A small smile gradually appeared on her young pink lips when she emerged from that fascinating world of thoughts and passing images. She then took a pause. Even at her intellectually tender age, she wondered at her experience with facets of reality, one so vastly different in character from the other. Yet the mind, grappling with the unravelling of the roof, instead found a better perspective to see them side by side with the most-telling and engaging reality.

She switched off the reading lamp by the side of her easy chair and got up. Instead of joining her mother in the kitchen—not indeed in connection with the matter she had concluded talking about with her Bua, not at all—on an impulse, she turned to the small prayer room of her mother's. She entered the room, leaving her slippers at the entrance and covering her head with her dupatta. The aroma of incense was still in the air since her mother had performed her pooja in the morning. She sat there quietly, not exactly praying. Once, at the entrance, she looked up at the image of Lord Krishna with a benign smile on his face. She, too, perhaps smiled slightly and then dropped her eyelids to the plate of offerings at the feet of the lord, containing a heap of flowers, incense in embers and a piece of milk sweet. She had neither prayed nor sought a boon for anything in particular. Yet, when she got up to go, she felt like all things had fallen in place and the whole world around her was balanced. In that buoyant state, she seemed to walk on air when she went to see her mother in the kitchen.

The whole kitchen seemed like an oven with cooking simultaneously taking place on two stoves. Vidya was laughing when she entered—for no particular reason, just happy—and dragged her mother by her sweat-drenched arm. She sat on a sofa, pulling her mother down alongside, facing the courtyard with a border hedge and a few breeze-blown trees, from one of which hung and slowly swung a rope swing with an adjustable narrow wooden seat about two feet above the ground.

'O, Mama! In this excess of work. You're spending so much more time in the kitchen, I know. You're overlaying anxieties by keeping physically busy in the kitchen or such other housework, which have otherwise been smoothly attended to by the help you have so wisely employed,' she began to dab her mother's flushed face with her soft and clean dupatta and wiped it dry. Vidya also brought some cheer and her naughty smile, 'Look into my eyes, Mama.' And with an imperceptible half wink, she continued, 'Don't you think that your daughter is grown up enough, and the people may accuse you of being remiss for not realizing that it's time she was sent packing off to her in-laws'?'

At this, she began to laugh, leaning on her mother's shoulder. Her mother, too, put her arms around her beloved Vidya. But the laugh turned into a sort of hiccup of a sob, which was followed by a trail of soft sobs and a profusion of tears. Both of them knew what they were thinking and talking about. But soon they calmed down and swiftly disengaged, ready to face each other, when they heard the shuffle of Champa's slippers approaching them as she emerged from the kitchen door.

She had come to clarify something about the dessert recipe planned for the afternoon meal from Bibiji (the lady of the house, Sushila, Vidya's mother). She sat on the carpet in front of the sofa where Vidya and her mother sat. She talked to her Bibiji about the kind of high, low or medium flame to cook the dessert. And she tried to understand at which stage to alter the strength of the flame and for how long. She stood up and, shaking her head, shuffled back to the kitchen.

Left to themselves, mother and daughter once again felt drawn to each other. Sushila felt greatly at peace, having sensed that all was settled so far as Vidya's consent to accepting the proposal from Bandepur was concerned. That, indeed, was a great relief for her. For the rest were tradition and ritual. The line was towed without question by all, big and small, in society. They abided by the established order without raising as much as a squeak of protest.

Of course, with the passage of time, the common man showed signs of being increasingly better informed and enlightened. And with those came the echoes of distant political voices about women's empowerment and reservations. The women soon began to claim and find fresh footholds and make inroads into the erstwhile, conventional, all-male bastions in new spaces they created for themselves. Indeed, it would yet be another half-century, maybe more—a wide margin must be set aside for the period of intervening hiccups—before the framework of the work culture and ambience of the workplaces would change for women to be accepted as equals, and gender-based considerations in public places to disappear without becoming a veritable obstruction in the routine of work. To view the world through the prism of habit makes even the most wonderful and beautiful world a stale old place.

The fabric of domestic life and culture, which designates a diamond-faceted place to women since the time of recorded history, would be dearly contentious to transgress and adjust with the oncoming kaleidoscopic changes in societal and official interaction. The practise of awareness and understanding may go a long way in facilitating the transition. The conditioned and hardened human orientation, the conglomerate of stock human responses, does not make it easier at all. Yet, great civilizations pass and cultures are amalgamated with massive demographic and other changes. These can be noticed even in the physical features of individuals.

Vidya had long black tresses, but her skin was fairer than the generally prevalent skin colour of the same geographical area and its ecological conditions. Vidya wore and styled her hair in twin braids that were long and heavy. But she had secretly desired to get them styled like the film star Kanan Bala, and now she thought it was time for her to be a replica of her favourite. Yet, no sooner did the thought cross her mind that she showed signs of her own discomfiture. Looking within, she often felt that she was slightly at variance from the general characteristics of the growing youngsters, teenagers or adolescents, whose thoughts were always tinged with a trace or two of naughtiness. Sometimes, she thought of herself as a hoary head on rather green shoulders.

Among others, her dear friend, Radha, complained to her about it when out on a picnic with friends in Edward Park. The park was on the city fringes, with green manicured grounds and shady neem, peepul and mango trees, and also with a swimming pool in the middle of the sylvan scene. The girls gave themselves up to the sport, the game of hide and seek they had devised and enjoyed themselves with great verve around a hillock. Vidya found an injured pigeon lying under a tree, flapping its wings in vigorous spasms, and ran straight towards it. She brought some water from a running tap, not far from the park canteen, in the cap of a thermos. She sat under a tree with the pigeon in her lap, caressed it, and crooned meaningless assuaging words. She felt its breast convulsing like madly racing bellows. She also noticed a stray cat going around the tree at some distance and shooed it away.

Almost everyone had noticed that, instead of going for the current fashion of wearing clothes in flamboyant colours and cut along fashionable lines, Vidya would, at all times, be seen, at home or out in the market, sedately dressed in rather simple and sober, but never cheap or clumsy, clothing without ever much caring about the fashions. Yet, her natural choice and sense of dress were such that even in her simple outfits, she left an impression on people of a refined person, if not quite sophisticated, with a taste that came from a naturally cultured mind.

When alone, she delved into her own mind to reckon with her propensities and shortfalls. And if, to her mind, the propriety of the situation required, she covered her head with her dupatta with natural and slick, almost unnoticeable, movements of her head and hands. There was something innate about her, she found, for her to never consider herself a drifter, submitting to be led like the dumb, driven cattle—the herd mentality. Of her own independent idea, she was of a firm disposition. She could never think of herself as a sulking crybaby or as a mulishly obstinate person, as some relatives rated her when she refused to join the family picnic. She smiled to herself when she recalled her cousin Sudhir, who could sulk over not being given the control of reins of the whole cosmos. Obedient and respectable towards her parents, Vidya equally venerated all elders. Never cramped by bigoted religious or communal considerations, she was always open-minded, ready to discuss and resolve any matter of dispute, and equally open to reason. She accepted any new idea or way of approach but never allowed herself to be browbeaten by some self-opinionated stiff-necked snob.

She also pondered over her peculiar attitude of looking at everything seriously, turning things over and over in her mind until she thought she had detangled every twist of an argument and found an answer to the last lingering question. She smiled at herself, knowing that hardly anyone among her friends or circle of acquaintances or relatives ever laboured over such cogitation about things as she did. She had seen people living life just moment to moment and day to day; in a moment leaving behind all without a thought, happy-go-lucky, and at the end of the day, reading from a popular joke book and sharing laughter with friends to go off to sleep. This was not her idea of living life. She sometimes thought that it was because she had spent most of her time at home in the company of her Bua and her Mama.

She enjoyed listening to her Bua's tales of a lifetime spent in the complexity of the joint family. Like connected warrens, their living quarters had grown with the expansion of the family. To learn about the lineage of relatives that peopled the same family house, in the house's dark corners and empty spaces, there still seemed to linger echoes of shrill baby's cries, subdued impassioned murmurings, and flitting spooky presences. She was ever keen to get a deeper insight into life and its attitudes and, most of all, into the relationships among them. It was only from her Bua's standpoint that she would visualize the passing caravan and get the pulse of life; she could sit for hours and listen to her Bua during her vacations. And later, she sat down to sort out these experiences and ideas and tried and place them in the perspective of the present-day's outlook. She found the practise quite strenuous but rewarding, for it gave her a better understanding of the reality then and now. But she listened to her Bua with great interest and attention, like a good pupil. Not only were the stories of gripping interest to her, being the history of her own family but they were also made engrossing by the graphic description of her Bua's narrative. She did sometimes feel that Bua didn't mind leaving a stamp of her personal biases on what she recounted from her memory. She spoke and told her tales with an assumed unimpeachable authority; Bua had been like that right from the time Vidya could remember. She left no room for others to question or gainsay whatever she said.

So, the innate strength of Vidya's character grew from strength to finer strength because she was endowed with the natural faculty of setting aside whatever she thought was irrelevant to her. Firm in her core, she also seemed to grow up mentally faster than most other girls her age. She could be graded and seen in the same maturity as her Bua. Indeed, girls do any day mature faster than boys, but Vidya was a class apart. She had that innate ability of the kind of independent thought, which like the gold leaves of the electroscope, is sensitive to the ideas and opinions floating around yet impervious to immediate influence. She took time but turned ideas around within her prism of thoughts until she was able to decide for herself what the essential reality was and what her response should be. This was perhaps the reason why she never complained about things going awry if and when they did.

Born to a very religious and upright man like her father, Vidya sometimes wondered how she could give herself to such prolixity of thought. Out of her natural custom, she hypothetically tried to gauge her friend Radha's attitude and concluded that Radha was more matter of fact—having taken a decision, she didn't remember her thinking or talking about the matter anymore. She just went the whole hog with her decision and enjoyed whatever ensued. Vidya, therefore, came to the conclusion about herself that she was something of an introvert and, perhaps, a wastefully pondering type. The intensity of her character was the result of this dimension of an analytic probing habit.

And she rested at that.

Even with regard to the prospects of settling down in marriage, she had come to the conclusion that if the endowments of her clear and strong mind had always given her the confidence to be able to successfully face the toughest challenge, whether academic or on the sports field, she was going to face the strange new world with the same élan.

As assets on her side, she counted her very highly educated and cultured partner for life, besides the blessings of all the elders and the benediction of the deity. Bolstered by such benign protective armour, she was ready with open arms to receive what her life had to offer. She could palpably feel a surge taking shape and rearing up within her.

6

It was his neighbour, Doctor Prakash Gulati, who first brought Vikramjit (or Vikram, as his friends called him) as a guest member to the club to spend an evening in the lively atmosphere of piano music from the dais at the corner of the hall; there was at least one vocal performance by the most popular singer in town, regarded by his stage appearance or in public concerts, Mr Raja Kapoor, who, for a change, invited a female voice to alternate him with, another popular singer from the Radio Station, Dolly Pinto. She was a junior artist who had launched her career as a singer of devotional songs, bhajans, in the early morning slot, from 6.00 a.m. to 6.30 a.m. And there were other activities that the club provided its members with, such as a billiard table, a card room attached to a bar and a supper counter. Being a handsome man, especially with his greyish blue eyes and his perfectly tuned outfit of light-blue shirts and dark trousers on a summer evening, Vikram at once drew the attention of

Ruby, whom he saw dancing with a nondescript young man, whom he later discovered was Ruben, the son of the manager of the club, Mohan Johnson.

Ruby, a Christian girl, was the daughter of Reverend Father William Constantine, Bishop of the local Catholic Church. Swarthy, tall and loose-limbed, the clergyman had a fleshy mouth and slight squint in his right eye, but he was very popular with his broad smile, like a permanent feature of this face, and was loved by his diocesans. Ruby Williams, his daughter, was employed as a senior maternity nurse in the only well-equipped hospital, Ford's Hospital, in the small town. Sometimes, on Saturday evenings, instead of going back straight from the hospital to her staid routine of going into the kitchen and baking a cake or some other savouries for the family (of which her father was the foremost admirer), she went to the club to break the monotony and sought a bit of excitement and adventure. And this wasn't a regular habit, but only depended upon the whim of the moment as she left Ford's after her duty hours.

Like her father, she was tall for an Indian woman, five three, with a pert nose and schoolgirl straight locks; and with the uniform complexion of her skin and curves at the right places, she was indeed pretty good-looking. She was well aware of her attractive appearance and the eyes that followed her swaying movements across the hall to the bar. Indeed, she was tickled to notice the kind of impression she made on the people around her. What made her appearance pleasant was the ready smile playing around her full Cupid's bow mouth. After her first dance number, a foxtrot quickstep, when Ruben had said his 'thank you', without much ado, she walked away alone in the direction of the drinks bar and bought a beer for herself. Sitting on the tall stool, she half turned round to cast a searching glance around. She was struck by the young man who sat by himself with his drink and half-smoked cigarette, sending up a wavy stream of smoke from the ashtray on his table.

Prakash had an appointment to keep and had sent a message that even if he could manage it, he'd still be a bit late. Vikram, who had been following Ruby from the corner of his eye, became conscious of his audacity, which could be counted as unmannerly in view of his position as the magistrate, and withdrew his eyes to look at the pianist playing from his raised corner.

After briefly contemplating her moves, Ruby slid down from her high stool with what seemed a definite mind to go ahead. She walked towards Vikram gracefully in her medium-high heels with a swing to her skirt, adding charm to her deliberately graceful walk. Although Vikram was vaguely aware of her approaching figure, he showed an appropriate degree of surprise when she bent and rather softly said, 'You mind if I join you at your table, Mister...'

'I'm Rana, Vikramjit Rana,' he stood up with a slight start. 'And I'm addressing?' He smiled a little and motioned for her to take her seat across the round table. 'Do sit down, please?' He pulled the chair slightly away from the table to make it convenient for her to sit down. And he added, when he saw her carrying her drink with her, 'You needn't have brought the drink with you. You are welcome, anyway.' And he smiled a little again, which she reciprocated broadly.

Vikram naturally had a sort of stern look around his eyes and a thin line for a mouth. Yet his smile, especially if seen for the first time, and more so if it happened to be seen by a good-looking young lady, had something of simple childlike innocence. Though his eyes still retained their shrewd power—unfathomable, like that of a policeman's, or holding profound wisdom of a weather-beaten, grizzled, wild mane.

Vikram was brusque and brief while introducing himself. 'I'm with the Justice Department and have my office in the district courts,' he said, bringing up his thin-lipped smile. He fell silent, waiting for her to come up with her own introduction.

She took the hint and said, 'I'm Ruby Williams, a staff nurse at Ford's Hospital. My father is a clergyman, Bishop of the local Catholic Church.' She moved to the edge of her chair and extended her hand, gesturing to shake hands with Vikram. He, in turn, took and shook her hand rather warmly for a first handshake and again smiled, showing his fine set of teeth and looking straight into her eyes. She felt as though she had missed a beat when she met his penetrating bluish eyes and felt the squeeze of his very masculine hand. And, spellbound for a moment, she delayed withdrawing her hand from his warm grip.

In a voice slightly raised due to a surge of eagerness, he began, 'What a coincidence! I know the doctor there, Doctor Gulati. Isn't he the Medical Officer, Administration, at Ford's Hospital? And yes, he may be coming to join me here any time now.'

He looked at his wristwatch.

'I'd be happy to see him out of the wards of the hospital,' she said, and all at once, she fished out her tiny handkerchief from her black leather handbag, covered her mouth, and smothered a loud laugh. She continued for a while.

Taken by surprise, Vikram didn't interrupt her, just smiled his small smile. And when she regained normal breathing, she told Vikram, 'I'm sorry, truly. It was quite idiotic, but I recalled the whole instance, and I do need to explain,' and she launched on her narration. 'You, sir, must have noticed that he has a rather unusually big nose and wide nostrils, and the girls are always quick to find anything ticklish and funny. It then becomes widespread. A few of the girls on staff had seen the movie *Cyrano de Bergerac*, the character who gets into all kinds of scraps and tiffs and, at times, has to face a duel because of the laughter his giant nose sparked in public. Loud-mouthed louts on the streets of Paris made nasty remarks that led to recriminations, squabbles and brawls. And worse still, they even ended up fighting real duels. So, privately among ourselves, we gave him the sobriquet "Cyrano". It is a kind of innocent joke over which we have some fun. But of late, it seems he has discovered the snuffed giggles among the batch of nurses that went on rounds with him through the wards. Let me assure you, it was meant as pure and simple fun, without a trace of intended sneer or insult. He is a very nice man and a great scholarly doctor in the classroom. We, the staff and the students, respect him.'

'I'm sure,' Vikram said, 'Someone like you would never

have joined a group that indulged in such atrociously vulgar mockery of a teacher.'

'How can you say something like that to a stranger? We've known each other for less than an hour.' She smiled coyly and dropped her eyelids, and examined her polished nails.

Vikram laughed, half a guffaw, and said, 'I do so by your very decision and then your ability to follow it with definite action. You have proved that something in your sixth sense, or intuition, indicated to you that coming over to join me, a total stranger at the table, should be all right, without hazards and hassles. And now, in my case, there's so much more besides intuition, which all human beings are endowed with—some with more and some with less sensitivity—and, along with my academic background, I have experience in scrutinizing all kinds of people in huge numbers. Every day of the week, I'm aided by the prosecutors and defence in their argument over complicated criminal cases. The defence definitely brings out the insidious aspects of a character, questioning the numerous witnesses. All this experience sharpens and refines the acumen of looking at people and immediately grasping and evaluating their character.'

'Now, now, please don't talk in such high-flying language that I begin to feel as though I'm reading from a book or attending a class lecture and need a dictionary within reach all the time,' she said and laughed.

Vikram joined in the laughter and, for a few moments, they forgot the club and the guests and got lost in mutual joy and its celebration. Their smiles were still lingering on their faces when the piano struck up a new number that happened to be a popular waltz from an earlier decade. At this, they looked up straight into each other's eyes and smiled. At the same time, she spotted Ruben striding towards the table that she was seated at, also with a smile and gesturing an enquiry if she'd give him the next dance as well. He came to the table and, with great élan, addressed Mr Rana by introducing himself. Rana, in turn, got up from his chair and briefly shook hands with him and smiled. Ruby kept on sitting and told Ruben that she had already promised Mr Rana the next dance, and she gave Rana a surreptitious glance.

'Later, perhaps,' said Ruben in self-assurance and walked back, where he still had a draught or two of beer left in his glass. He started off from where he had left with his friends and almost didn't care to hear that 'Perhaps' wasn't what Ruby said in reply.

Vikram noticed that her tall beer glass was empty and asked her if she'd care to have it replenished. 'Shall I summon the waiter?'

'Yes,' she said. 'I'd love to have another beer,' and she added, 'If only to stretch the joy of being in your company. But I thought you overheard when I told Ruben that I had pledged my next dance to you. Let's, please, have this short piece of cutting a figure on the floor before we return to finish our drinks.'

'Sure,' he said, 'Let's get to know each other better. Physical proximity does have its own magic. The vibes can either synchronize and sing in unison or repel each other with some mystic power. Thus, I believe lifelong relationships are formed or just missed to be formed. Put into words, I don't know how the meaning would go across to you. But by the end, when there's a fusion of music, dance and the human element, it stirs the whole being as a single clap of thunder can, proving an experience to enlighten both. Yes or no gets clearly writ.'

At every change over to a slower pace—one, two, forward or backwards, sideways of three, four, of their waltzing steps—their bodies came closer, and he felt the grip of her hand tightening, coinciding with the momentary and deliberately applied pressure of her breast. Vikram noticed this tantalizingly happened twice in consecutive movements. He just played ball. He didn't want to jolt her with any sudden moves. The move, in fact, came from Ruby when she allowed her firm breasts to graze past him and prolonged the moment by a fraction, sending her signals during the next step for a sideway move. Vikram responded right away, slightly increasing the pressure of his right arm that enclosed her waist. A deep rosy flush arose on her cheeks as she looked up into his eyes and smiled; together, their smiles were blissful.

The waiter, who seemed to have been waiting for them to return to their table, briskly came and bent lowly to Vikramjit Rana and told him in a loud whisper, 'Gulati Sahib rang up to talk to you and when told that you were on the dance floor, he left a message for you that, he may, after all, not be able to come at all and would see you tomorrow.'

'Thank you, Harish, thank you,' said Vikram to the waiter, who then turned on his heels and went back to his fold.

He stepped back and bowed gracefully. Ruby and he began walking back to their table.

The suggestion came from Vikram. 'If you're not really keen to go back home, let's get back to our drinks on the table, enough I hope to last us to sit and talk for another half hour.'

'Okay,' she said, looking at her teeny-weeny wristwatch. 'Let it be just that, a half hour and no more. I don't like being shouted at by my mom as though I'm still a kid at twenty-two.'

They settled down with their drinks and began opening up and sharing their travelling experiences—long and short journeys during holidays with families or friends, trekking into the hills. Gradually, the confabulations drifted into sharing their peculiar likes and dislikes of things in common day-to-day life. And they were not a little surprised to find how much they had in common. And thus, in the newfound intimacy of the not-very-brightly lit clubhouse, the time flew past, and they were hardly aware of it.

And when, with a typically feminine pout, Ruby complained that getting back home so late, she would be ready prey for her mother, Vikram gave a reassuring pat on her shoulder and said, 'I'll escort you and talk to your father about the reasons behind your having been so late and maybe talk you out of an unpleasant altercation.'

He gestured to Harish, waiting in the wings, to come to him. He sent a message to his driver to get the car out at the exit. 'Now, wipe the extra shine off your nose and powder it to look normal, and let's walk out without any signs of fluster or haste.'

Outside, the car door was opened by Om, the driver;

Vikram lent Ruby the support of his hand to get into the seat. He went round to the entrance on the other side to sit beside her. It was an Austin 8, black in colour. Vikram gave Om instructions about the destination and route before he put the purring engine into gear and took off.

In the small area that Gujarat covered, Om knew where the church was and the entrance to the rectory. It was just about 10.30 p.m. when the car came to a halt in front of the doorstep of the church house.

Ruby delicately tapped the door knocker twice and stood back, teetering on the first step.

Preventing the Rector from starting any unpleasant enquiries, Vikram very diplomatically took a step forward and wished the hoary-headed clergyman in his surplice and skullcap a 'good evening' with a reverential bow and introduced himself. The clergyman, learning of his untimely guest's high-ranking position in the district, received him with his full-lipped and broad smile, blemished only by his slight squint. In spite of the late hour, the bishop asked him to come inside for a while. Ruby excused herself from the company in the sitting room, said, 'I'll be back,' and disappeared into the interiors of the house. After a minute of whispers with her mother, she went into the toilet to refresh herself.

In the meanwhile, Ruby's mother joined her father in the sitting room with Vikram. When she found her husband persuading Vikram to have a bite of a seed cake that their daughter had baked, she promptly but quietly went inside to her sideboard to bring in a wholesome wedge of a chocolate cake on a florally-edged china plate.

Placing it on the table, she said in an undertone to her husband, 'Pour a glass of Port for the young man, why don't you?'

While the husband went inside to the sideboard, which was also used as the family bar, Alva Constantine sat facing Vikram and began conversing with him.

'Ruby is hardly ever late; and if she is, it is by at the most a half hour, when sometimes she makes a stopover at the club, along with her friend, Loyola of the Bose family in the neighbourhood, whom we all know well. We are never worried about her. Also, she knows their common friend, so to say, Ruben Williams, who she has told us is the son of the club manager and is almost a fixture during the evenings. God alone knows where he finds time for his studies. He's at the University in the Department of Economics, studying for an honour's degree. And for his habitual sponging, he's known as being a hanger-on!' She heard the shuffle of her husband's bedroom slippers and began urging upon the unexpected but decent guest to have a bite of the cake and get a taste of Ruby's baking. 'Her father is extremely proud of the cakes and pastries baked by his daughter, some of which she bakes almost every other day.'

'And here is some Port to wash it down with. It is from Burgundy, courtesy of an old friend who owns a vineyard there and sends a case during the season,' Father Constantine came in saying.

There was no way Vikram could get out of the corner he'd been driven into by his own goodness and culture. Nonetheless, by the lurking memory of the sharp sprouts of desire that had almost possessed him, he had to prolong his stay at Ruby's home, which may make him a bit more expansive. Going by propriety, he thought, it was the right thing to do. That is, to go over the events of the evening for the family before they begin to draw their own conclusions. Not only would it clear the air for now, but also prevent a crop of misunderstandings from taking root at any later time. He suddenly became conscious of his status, which in turn made him realize that he needed to take care of his communications in local society; his conduct must always be above reproach and, even casually, he must never let any occasion arise for even a trace of blemish to colour his image, inside or outside of the courts. This could cast a shadow on the daunting authority of his official position. He had to maintain his dignified place and apposite distance from the commonality.

Turning the matter over, his inwardly examined and approved conclusion was that it would be appropriate for him to go along for, say, fifteen minutes and get over the cliff rather than carry an evitable tangled ball of wool in his mind. He had better things to do, other ridges to climb and go across.

'O, Reverend Sir, you didn't need to fuss so much over this and so late in the evening. On the contrary, I need to apologize to you for having disturbed your peace,' said Vikram, and continued, 'It's perhaps on two counts that I owe an apology. Let me explain. I contributed to Ruby's being late. My friend the doctor, Dr Gulati, who is the Medical Officer at Ford's and Ruby's boss, as I was told during our repartee...

Yes, it was this casual exchange of experiences and ideas between the two of us and a dance Ruby so graciously agreed to have with me while I waited for my friend to join me, which he finally didn't...he couldn't because of an emergency engagement with an old patient. One thing led to another. She told me a story about my doctor friend, over which we had a good laugh. For a while, we were engrossed in small talk until I sensed that Ruby was fidgety, and I asked her the reason. At that moment, she indicated that she should not be getting so unpardonably late lest she should get a dressing down from her mother, and especially said that at her age, she should mind her conduct. She shouldn't give her mother any reason to get anxious and fret,' shakily, he wound up his circuitous confabulation on a high note.

'I felt guilty, and even though our acquaintance was brief, I felt it was my duty as atonement to escort her back home and own up to my share of fault in her getting delayed in returning home. The long and short of it is that Ruby is a good, simple and honest person. After meeting you, I can visualize the halo of the cultured family background that surrounds her and which she exudes, and I have reason to hope our friendship would be of a lasting kind. That was another reason I took it upon myself to bring her back to her family myself.'

He would have perhaps gone on when Ruby made a brief appearance, keeping her eyes lowered, and gave a passing glance at her father and Vikram before she went back inside after she had said 'good night' to them both.

Her mother was waiting to give her a bit of supper and a

word or two of motherly advice to be careful, and she, too, left the sitting room to her husband and their guest. Husband and wife saw their guest off at the door after 'good nights' and 'bye byes' and promises of continuing to keep in touch.

7

Vikram had a small smile on his thin mouth. He was happy with the way things had gone. But he was reminded out of the blue of his childhood friend, Pappo, short for Pratap. Vikram made a strange gesture of turning his head right and left to see if he was not really around. Pappo had, after completing graduation from the Distance Education Department of the University of Delhi, started a small property dealers' business, which was just the right choice for his 'sharpshooting' temperament, and his foxy ways smoothly fell in step with the marketplace of shrewd underhand dealings. Pappo had always been a sort of foil to his friend's poker-faced claims ever since they flew kites and spun tops together on the brick-laid uneven streets of Bandepur—playing the Fool to King Lear, puncturing his windbag.

Vikram was quite sure that the situation, all that he had said and the manner in which he had said it would have given Pappo a tickle in his side, rousing his funny bone. This was reason enough for his straggling shadow to appear from behind a door to briskly catch up with him, down to the car, and with suppressed laughter, to say something to the effect, 'What the hell do you think you are doing, hey, Vicky? With your smooth tongue and smoother mannerisms, are you trying to dupe the poor holy man and the lady, earnestly playing the mother to your lately chosen girlfriend, who, too, you tried your sleight of duping hand on? You tongue-in-cheek lover!'

And in the car, as Om began driving him back home, several images from his past while studying law in England flashed in his mind. Vikram had met Molly Massey in the Christ Church Hospital where he was admitted for a general check-up due to unrelieved cough and fever over a couple of weeks. He had had to keep his mouth open for a while so that the nurse, Ms Massey, could thrust a rubber tubing into his mouth, all the way to his stomach, to get a sample for a stomach wash to rule out the serious bacilli infection of tuberculosis. After her manoeuvres, she smiled to take the edge off the discomfort she had caused and boldly remarked that he had a fine set of teeth. She was perhaps conscious of her own double upper canine riding the other, which raised her upper lip slightly on the right side.

Vikram smiled and thanked her for the compliment. He then went on to ask her name in spite of the unmannerly audacity of the gesture. He was relieved to see she didn't take it amiss and turned round to smile at him, looking straight into his bluish eyes.

The stomach wash had to be cultured and the test took around ten days. His telephone jangled, and he was glad to hear Molly calling and greatly relieved to learn that he had been cleared of all suspicion of infection. He thanked her effusively and asked her if it would be improper to ask for her telephone number to call her up sometime. She demurred and said as much to him. She indicated that her duty hours were at all kinds of odd times. She didn't get a break at a decent time of the day. But he was not listening to her.

'Oh, I won't pester you; if not for lunch, we could sometime go to the Ritz for dinner. They're open till late. I believe until 2.00 a.m. I can always walk you safely back to the hospital.' He laughed and left it for her to take it the way she preferred.

From their brief exchanges on the phone and after getting together at the Ritz whenever their free time coincided and suited them, Molly decided that Vikram was a decent man with refined tastes. And this awakened her trust in his goodness. She agreed and started going to his digs whenever she had a day or an evening off from her duties at the hospital. The intimacy and proximity in the privacy of his room inevitably grew into a closer physical relationship. This continued, becoming almost a habit. The emotion of love never happened to pass their lips in expressive words, but there seemed to exist something of the sort as an undercurrent in the ongoing relationship, although how seriously Vikram took it was anybody's guess.

So, it wasn't much of a shock to him when Molly walked out on him, sending him a note by post after she had noticed him walking on the lawns of Middle Temple with his arm around Maud's waist, bent towards her and giggling and talking intimately. To rub it in further, Molly told him to send her back all the mementoes she had given him by Value Payable Post and promised to send him all he had gifted her.

He *had* started being friendly and was cosying up to Maud of late. Molly had noted it at one of the Saturday evening dance parties two days ago at the Ritz. But she had returned to her hospital room, and cried bitterly over the disenchantment of her faith in Vikram; appalled to have seen him in that state of intimacy with another woman. She felt worse when she saw her nose and eyes crimson in the looking glass on the wall. She hurried into the toilet, sluiced her eyes and face, and dabbed it dry to be prepared to meet any chance visit from a colleague.

In a few more months and Vikram would be through with his final term in the Middle Temple to be a fully qualified barrister. Quite aware of and ever focused on his aim and object, to the expectation of the people way back home, he worked diligently to make it among the top five of those who would pass out from the Middle Temple qualified.

Indeed, he made it.

He was placed third. In spite of giving way to his wayward urges and letting himself go to have passing flirtations, and even an affair or two of philandering that lasted a week or a full moon (and according to him, not worth the mention), Vikram never lost sight of the serious purpose for which he had been sent to England by his father. Being a calculating son of a trading father, a Brahmin by birth, he assigned his pleasurable pursuits in their proper place as a passing entertainment, not to intrude or disrupt the scheduled regimen of his pursuit to earn his graduation from the Middle Temple and bring glory to the family back home. Considering his education and intelligence, his letting himself go and taking a bite from the pie of dissolute life may have been because of a personal desire to gain experience of human behaviour in a section of society in addition to a degree in law.

Vikram was clearly laying the foundations for a successful career to culminate in prosperity and a life of luxury for all his progeny. All his energy and efforts were aimed in this direction. He smiled secretly, therefore, whenever a partner of his jaunts used the word 'love' for their impassioned but passing relationships. For Vikram, the word 'love' could properly be used only in filial contexts—between a child and his parents. He considered his relationships a mutually understood commercial code—an exchange of favours. Like buying a packet of cigarettes, you choose your brand and pass the money over the counter, and the pack is yours so long the cigarettes last. There's no scope for any grouse once the cigarettes have gone up in smoke, nor of any lurking belated hope. 'If only the time of burning out drags could have been stretched'—leaving behind its potential of causing malignancy—when you have had your pleasure that was already paid for. Through his tortuous experiences, the lesson was loud and clear that human life in this world, in this whole phantasmagoria, was merely a huge marketplace of jostling multitudes; every glittering thing had a price tag that had to be paid for if you wanted to own any part of it for your exclusive use.

Indeed, there is a wide margin for those who have mastered the machinations of the market, for the arena of exploitation leaves the weak pitted against the strong, physically or financially, allowing the predator room enough to lay his trap. No Lenin or Lincoln has ever been able to do anything substantially lasting about it; referred to as 'fair play' by the cynic. Such contemptuous or derisive voices have always appeared as bolts of lightning to pulverise the normal or even-looking skies.

With Ruby, Vikram thought, here in the slow-paced life of Gujarat, with the traditional values still holding, with doddering, bowed and hoary figures still moving in the streets and the marketplace among the next generation, their faces lit with the grace of old age, it was, *perhaps,* different. From the perspective of another look, it might turn out to be a mere wishful thought. But it was a wishful thought worth nurturing, for it contained a vision of heaven, cleared of the rebel angel Lucifer and his comrades, now in the dungeons of eternal perdition. He thought he even had a hologram-like glimpse of such a vision when he had manoeuvred himself as a guest in the household of Father Constantine. He was unsure whether there had been a remote undercurrent of motivation besides what was so tangibly true, of which he was a tangible part. In fact, he liked to believe that Father Constantine's church militant may not exactly be the true image of the church triumphant; but being its representation in the temporal world, the flaws streaked across and were inherent in its creation. He, therefore, also liked to believe that the not-so-tangible entity, commonly termed as 'love', of having felt over the evening of being in emotional unison with Ruby, too, was true. It did manifest the power to drive Vikram through the events that had played out during this very evening.

In bed, he began turning matters such as these in his mind over and again, pertaining to the advent of his relationship with Ruby. Her image and a heart-warming quiet returned to settle his mind in favour of the sunshine-filled experience he associated with her very presence. Her company and his experience of the whole evening, too, buttressed the emotion; he hoped it was shared and wasn't one-sided on his part. This momentarily made him lose his quiet, but then he made up his mind. Yes, he thought there wasn't anything better than plain-speaking. The uncertainty of cogitations and this guessing game of plucking petals, for which he had no stomach, would upset him, and more than that, it would be a drag on his magisterial work during the days the indecision lingered.

Nursing, a round-the-clock job, comprised eight-hour shifts for each nursing sister. Ruby secretly waited for the shift when she had two consecutive evenings to herself and could take a detour to the club instead of making a beeline back home. Vikram knew Ruby's duty schedule by heart. On the days she had her evenings to herself, she invariably made it to the club to be in the company of Vikram, for whom her fondness grew by the day and strengthened after every meeting. And Ruby could always find pretexts and means to increase the frequency of their meetings. They had begun to find the occasions of their meetings become sparse and short; always leaving them desiring more. He was, indeed, taken somewhat by surprise when one evening she was held up at the hospital and got late reaching the club, where she knew Vikram would be waiting for her. For, he too, due to the increase in the volume of work at his office, part of which he had had to bring home to complete, could not see Ruby whenever he so wanted; and both waited until they could decide upon a mutually convenient day.

The cumulating intensity of emotion and desire fuelled her to what the sticklers of morality may consider boldness, but out of all simplicity, she placed her hand on his arm as she sat next to him on the sofa and said, in a rather choked and soft voice, 'Do you think, Vikram, it would be out of place for me to sometime come to your rooms to see you there? Otherwise, I can hardly wait for the occasion. The intervening time stretches like a desert and I, like a tired and thirsty traveller, stare at the distant hazy horizon. Come on, say yes. I know you want to but for some stray hypothetical reasons. I know you have the answers to all your apprehensions.'

Indeed, Vikram, though conscious of the proprieties pertaining to his official status and his honourable place in society, was apparently reluctant but was glad to consent to her coming to visit him in his rooms.

He knew that two members of his staff, the cook, Neeta, and the cleaner boy, Raju, would be the first to raise their eyebrows. His driver, Om, was already familiar with his employer's relationship with Ruby, but Prabhu, the official attendant he was provided with by the Court, who also helped with his household chores of sorts, too, would be no less curious about the new visitor. More so because Ruby, at times without realizing how the servants of the house would take her demeanour, went about overseeing arrangements like she was the lady of the house due to her confidence in her devotion to Vikram. She did so because of the all-enveloping bond of intimacy that had grown between Vikram and her, and from the intimacy came freedom, which devolved into authority. The staff thought that she talked to them as though authority had been officially delegated to her, and perhaps they were not able to deduce that it had naturally ensued from her closeness to their master, whose stamp it therefore bore.

Since she started visiting and spending time with Vikram in his flat, the servants had noticed and understood the nuances of their equation as it evolved, and without being explicitly told, they complied with the shift of authority. Vikram didn't consider it necessary to spell anything out to his staff in particular. Gradually, during Ruby's presence in the house, the undertones of change in the behaviour of the staff indicated clearly enough that they were adjusting to the change that was palpably felt in the atmosphere of the household. Her ubiquitous presence was a generally accepted thing. The due deferential attitude was evident in the conduct of everyone.

Even Vikram's visits to the Constantine household became frequent. On almost all his days off, unless preoccupied officially or by another social engagement, it was understood that he would have his lunch or dinner with Ruby's family, especially on festival days like Christmas or Easter, when gifts too were exchanged.

Alva chiefly looked forward to his visits. She had grown fond of him and spent long hours recounting and sharing minute little events and feelings with him. He could feel her sheer affection as she took him into confidence, but was left not a little surprised when she hugged him closely and surreptitiously. Though over the period of a year and more, as familiarity grew into that of a familial relationship, she had dropped hints about their intention of getting their daughter married outside of their faith and community if there were no adverse considerations from the bridegroom's Brahmin family. He took the hint that he must probe the matter at his own end and bring the family around to agree to accept a situation in direct confrontation with social anathema.

The Constantines, at home, had thought about the matter and placed their daughter's happiness as a top priority. They were glad never to have seen Ruby morose or sulking, locked in her room for long hours, all during her association with Vikram. They were content to notice that things were sailing at an even keel. Besides, Vikram was quite competent in dealing with exigencies and in bringing matters under his control, settling matters to everybody's satisfaction. His diplomacy never lost sight of fair play and justice according to the spirit of the law.

So much had happened, so much was happening, and his lassitude was such that he had not been able to talk to his friend, Dr Gulati, by whose graciousness he had access into the club where he had met Ruby, who had now come to mean so much to him that he could not think of his life without her presence. And yet he lagged in giving an update to Gulati. It had to be no less than a solemn confession, to which a footnote of an apology needed to be added as he saw his conduct in his hindsight. He had to make a clean breast of much more than merely as a friendly gesture. Vikram tended to consider even the tiniest exchange in terms of the value of the relationship. For him, therefore, it was an obligation that far outweighed saying 'thank you' or 'sorry' to settle all accounts. He thus made it a point to meet Gulati at the club and to sit at the corner table and own up to all that was permitted by propriety regarding his relationship with Ruby since the day he had met her.

Vikram reminded Gulati of the day when his absence left him with time on his hands. It was on that fateful day, things transpired as they did, and then they evolved. And it was as though godsend all that followed. After a long harangue of about an hour, in which he tried to make things clear to Gulati, he felt his mind lightening and cleared of a cloud of guilt. It all amounted to what commingled as his confessional and justification of the inevitability and which too was gone by and sealed.

He had to do the same, perhaps much more—a plan he yet had to carry out—with the people at home, and especially his father, who was emotionally attached to him. He decided to carry out his resolve in the very next break he would take at home. The very thought of getting things settled brought his perturbed mind to rest and also made him apply himself better to work at courts, which he hadn't been able to do for some time. There was yet the Rubicon to be crossed. So, when he met Ruby in the club on Saturday, he told her they would go to his rooms. She was happy. But when she saw Vikram's face darkened by an ominous cloud, she stopped short of all her speech; her joy was throttled, but the apprehensive questions that rose in her mind were quelled. Everything else seemed to be as usual, and she felt his arm around her waist still had the same warmth as he led her to the car.

The matter was so delicate that, though he had turned it in his mind several times, he was still not sure how to put it across to her so as not to give her a jolt or move her to tears. That, he thought, would be most unfortunate.

In spite of their close relationship and total mutual agreement on little matters, there was something delicate about their relationship, which he dreaded shaking up by a lightning bolt, with a topic that he was going to bring up with her. After all, she had staked her life, willingly going deeper and deeper into their relationship on her deep faith in the veracity of Vikram's word and character as a whole. He would not trivialize his love for her. In fact, she didn't remember his having referred to their relationship in a casual or frivolous vein at any time.

She was confirmed in her faith in his abiding devotion. When she studied the expression in his eyes closely for hours after she had told him, never meant to be blamed, that he had taken her, known her and in God's eyes, she was his wife and he was her husband—until death did them part—yes, never for a moment had she found the light wavering from his eyes.

He had said, 'Oh yes, my darling Ruby, yes, and yes, a thousand times.'

The bond had been strengthened and sanctified, though by no mundane priest. 'There is a spirit...,' he had said, '...in the human heart, which is a judge above all other judges—a true judge. He stands ever bowed and humble before that judge, dauntless, ready to be arraigned but steady in the knowledge of having been in no act of transgression. It would truly be an act of offence, had any fraction inside you revolted. Your whole being, I felt, did not move with a single vibration embodying revulsion to what blossomed as the piety of love's extension, and therefore, could it go on, until the breeze lifted the curtains from the window and the foliage of the neem wafted in the bliss of the unison in the heavenly breeze and the terra-rooted tree.'

On the settee, he shifted slightly away from the fold of her arm and nuzzling mouth. She looked at him a bit bewildered, but she had never seen him deliver his verdict in court when he looked at the facts of a case objectively, with the perspective of distance. Such was the face he turned towards her; for indeed, he was about to tell her something to which she, as an individual, would have mixed reactions, to begin with. Although he was going to be as much affected by the change, he perceived it was going to overtake their life. The subject matter was grave, and he had given it a lot of thought, but he kept his voice level and, to bring cheer to Ruby, let a constant smile hover round his lips. And with a reassuring pat on her shoulders, he began to give the news and also explain.

'Promise to hear me out with patience and with all the faith you have shown in me in all things we've gone through together. There is a reason I'm asking you to muster all our patience and faith. The matter is such that it is going to cause a change in our life for the rest of our time. Let such words not take your breath away. For you can take me to be there with you, at every place and every moment of our life—if not physically, I truly shall be, in spirit.'

'I don't know why you should be lingering over it. Come on, spill it out. I'll begin to have goosebumps with apprehension.'

'Don't push it, my dear. I'm trying not to give you a shock. Because I think it may be quite traumatic for you. And what I'm trying to prevent is that if you are prepared for the worst, it may not turn out to be as bad after all. The crux of the matter is that you and I must be married right away. It shall have to be a soft-pedalled and private affair up the aisle of your revered father's church. I shall beg of him to complete the ceremonies to his full satisfaction—we mustn't deprive ourselves of the benediction of heaven and blessings of the son of God—and yet, it must be a hush-hush procedure. We must not allow a word of it to be breathed out of the walls of the cathedral. Another life of a whole family, whom I deeply care about, would be at stake.

'Just be patient. Bear with me and hear me out. For more than a week now, I've been terribly perturbed. Twice in the last week, I've been assailed by letters from my father.

The second followed at the heels of the first because the first one was not responded to, which had never happened before. The first letter actually contained the seminal matter. It not only broke the news to me but also, in a single stroke, unhinged my whole being on the first impact. Through Herculean effort, I recovered from the big bang and then brought my wits under control and my thoughts to focus on the present reality. I saw the conundrum I faced. I had to sort out two matters close to my heart, which had bombed my brain into mangled confusion. You must forgive me for the mixed metaphors, which I believe are the result of the same explosion in my mind. And may, perhaps, be the cause of an ironic smile.

'Well, the fireball of news, the operative part, my father's first letter carried was is this—it is with utmost urgency your mother and I want you back home. It sounded to me no less than a 'do or die' situation. And then, within three days, another letter stressed the urgency, especially from my mother's side, as though my father's word was not enough. For appeasement, I sent them a wire and followed it up with a letter explaining that the arrangement of a leave of absence and other related matters would take routine time. But I assured them that I would be there at the earliest date. My mind was disturbed with apprehensions. I had been getting some inkling that, soon after my assuming office here, when my father came here to oversee the arrangements on my domestic front and returned, my mother and the rest of the family got busy looking for a bride for me to come and take over my welfare so that my digs should be a proper home, rounded off by a caring bride. My apprehension is that something has materialized from their efforts of search. I am preparing myself for the worst. I might find myself cornered. It is like carrying a monkey on my back. Social and family obligations aren't to be taken casually. Trivializing the family or the community's tradition is looked down upon, and reprisal may come as ostracism, like the sword of Damocles, threatening me. Life in the country is still quite hidebound by orthodoxies. If I go along with it in some way, it is out of my sheer love for my parents.

'Now you can understand the haste I am speaking of in finalizing our marriage ceremony. I have to feel assured that I have not left you in the lurch. I am going to see your revered father tomorrow, briefly explain the circumstances and, on my knees, seek your hand. Request him to get the ceremony over at the earliest. I know it will cause a flutter in the family and the community, but it is unnecessary for everyone to be invited except a few trusted folks. The intention, as you can understand, is that the love and faith you trusted me with must not suffer abrasions. You mustn't lose faith and patience during my absence. And doubt not, I shall never allow anything to deprecatingly reflect on our relationship that I've always considered piety.'

By the end of what Vikram said, he saw Ruby had her big beautiful eyes heavy-lidded and full of tears, just beginning to trickle down her cheeks. Her face had grown gaunt at the moment, and they left the whites of her eyes streaked with inflamed, red vessels. She was trying her utmost not to break down, yet couldn't check a long choking sob, accompanied by a moan, from escaping her. She had never doubted the veracity of Vikram's unwavering love for her but had also never anticipated such a calamitous exigency to arise and, like a bolt of lightning, shatter her 'dome of the many-splendoured universe'.

Vikram didn't try to stop her from letting go but held her close to him, not saying much but caressing her. The shock and grief peaking to decline till peace gradually returned to her. He put his arm around her waist and led her to his bedroom. After about an hour and more, when he found her breathing normal and steady, he told her to go use the toilet and freshen up so he could drive her back home. He left her at the doorstep and didn't go in with her. He would be coming to see her father the next day; he reminded her. But made sure that she didn't allow her emotions to get the better of her good sense. He reassured her of his abiding support at all times and situations, which she, in her heart, had never ever doubted.

She lifted her chin and walked in.

Vikram had put in his application for a leave of absence from his court soon after receiving his father's letter. He also deputed the office clerk to get his reservation on the connecting train to Sonepat for the next Monday. He had reckoned that all he had to get done before leaving Gujarat should be finished in the intervening eight days. The most essential part of the agenda for him was to be able to impart consolation and stability to the mind of his dearest Ruby, who he knew would be the most affected by his departure and absence. He could vicariously feel for her. She had become so much a part of his life that he, too, wondered how he was going to survive the duration of his separation from her. Besides, how was he going to conduct himself normally, as though all was tickety-boo? While he was carrying a choking lump deep in his breast? While going about among his family in the general mood of rejoicing for him and his forthcoming marriage? The prodigal had to play the 'sonny-good-boy' of his father. And the countdown for him had started now. He must persevere, especially for the sake of his greatest concern, Ruby, his delicate sweetheart, whom he could hardly bear to see with tears welling up in her beautiful eyes.

Less than ten days he had to himself, and he felt them the next morning as soon as he awoke. It came bearing down on his mind that even his body, as much as his mind, felt cramped. He was without any drive to take on all that while planning. He seemed to have accomplished it as soon as he had the blueprint in his mind. No wonder, therefore, the poet T.S. Eliot in his brief, witty utterance, said, 'between the idea; and the reality; [...] falls the shadow'. It is the human element; the inexorability of the course of the natural flux of things. And yet, the obstinacy of man is that he plans the best that he can and makes an effort at fulfilment. And does by his persistence attain his goal; though he is maimed and bleeding. He takes on the battle fully prepared and in full awareness.

In his rather slow and deliberate movements, he gave himself to turning over and rehearsing his encounter with Father Constantine. It would indeed be a very delicate situation and would call for equally careful handling. Vikram knew exactly what he was going to say to Ruby's father so that her status and her place in the hearts of her family members remained totally unexposed to any danger of being singed by an incendiary condition if any such was created, by what he planned to bring up in his conversation. He took his time to shave, shower and breakfast in order to time his reaching Ruby's residence only around the time when her father would be free after the matins. To inform Father Constantine of his coming to meet him, he had sent a short note through Pappu, who rode his bicycle to the church house to be quick.

Vikram saw that coffee things were laid out for four on the small round table in the sitting room when he rang the bell and was let in by Alva herself. Her broad smile and plump cheeks, he thought, were very inviting. He bent slightly forward and kissed her on both sides of her face and returned her smile, not without added naughtiness. Then he walked inside, side by side with her. Father Constantine stood up from his chair and shook hands with Vikram.

Cheerily, Vikram, even from a distance, had called out, 'Good morning, Sir.' Constantine reciprocated with added warmth and exchanged morning greetings, far advanced into the day though the morning was.

Ruby, from behind the curtain, entered the sunlit morning room. Her drooping eyelids showed that she had had an almost sleepless night. And although she smiled and greeted Vikram with as normal a face as she could muster, he knew the kind of predicament they were in. Now, he had come to push her parents too—being her parents, they were fated to—into sharing the same condition. Vikram had a compelling moral obligation to come clean of things considering the coils of time tightening and tugging around him.

She poured coffee for everyone and left the room on the pretext of making a phone call to her chief, the doctor at Ford's. Choking on a tumult of emotions, she was not sure she was going to be able to face her parents as the somewhat discomfiting aspect of her life was going to be revealed, however cautiously, by Vikram. Because of their wisdom, her parents may understand a part of it, but another part would, more as admission than revelation, be spoken by Vikram, however circuitously he may go about it.

Not wanting to waste any time, Vikram took the cue and addressed both her parents, particularly directing all he had to say to her father. His purpose was not to leave even a trace of misgiving in the minds of Ruby's parents so that, later, there may not, on any account, develop any strain between Ruby and her parents in his absence. He was sitting next to Alva. He casually placed his hand on hers that lay on the curved armrest of the chair.

He mustered the needed unction and said, 'Please do forgive me if you find anything untoward in what I say, for there's no offence meant. I only hypothetically pre-empt at a speech to iron out the folds of apprehension, if there are any. So I am not going to go over and recount the evolving depth of mutual liking and trust between Ruby and me. For, in your mature wisdom, it could not escape your notice and understanding, much more than you'd like others to believe. Therefore, it was great solace that Ruby came to meet me without hindrance. Such was your quiet assurance to me and unfettered freedom given to Ruby in this context. And therefore, I would be only reiterating the obvious that your lovely daughter and I are truly in love. And not leaving anything to speculation and apprehension, I made sure by asking her if she would be ready to accept me, as she had over months come to know me and be married to me. And I gave her enough time to ponder before making up her mind and replying. I was on tenterhooks for more than a fortnight.

'Let me explain to you how the matters came to a head and how it was precipitated by a letter from my father back home in Bandepur—especially the urgency of the content, which made me feel apprehensive. But Ruby's positive response resolved the most difficult part of my predicament. I sensed from the letter that there was something afoot in my hometown, about getting me married off into a family well known to ours down the generations. My affections, I was certain, had roots elsewhere. I was determined to abide by my inmost promptings—tacit avowals between Ruby and me had gained strength more than all other obligations and allegiances. And I would have unpardonably failed on every count had I dithered or wavered. I am sorry I cannot put it across better.

'It took me some time before I could bring my mind to focus and understand what was happening to me and around me, in the backdrop of the rest of the world. And I held the letter from my father in my hand. I shook my head with some nervous vigour to see right. So I decided to move ahead. Ruby's clear and truthful mind has made my task easier. Let me admit frankly that, in all that I am about to say to you, there may be several points that you may find it vexing to hear me state the obvious when you hardly need to be reminded, and as at such other points, where you may wonder and gape at my repetitiveness and long-windedness. What I can say is that perhaps it just reflects the state of my mind. Kindly forgive my youth and my inexperience. Indeed, I laugh at myself for this protracted monologue with which I'm weighing you down.'

He drew a long breath and paused before he resumed his nervous utterance. 'I thank God, though, for the cool that I could keep in that tense moment of hurry and all the rest when I decided what I did. What remains, therefore, is your kind goodwill. Bless my heart! Besides, of course, the church to sanctify our relationship with the benediction of heaven on the family, presuming you, sir, do not have any reservations on religious or other such social grounds. On my knees, here (and he bent on his right knee), I make bold to beg the hand of Ruby, your daughter, in marriage. And though I'm at present not supported by any elders of my family, I am fully answerable for their support to be forthcoming in favour of my proposition whenever reassurance is needed. And let me assure you, sir, that the happiness of Ruby and her lifelong personal and domestic comforts will always be my concern. (He rose, stood upright on his feet, and continued as he went to his chair and took his seat.) I hope you believe me on the grounds of your wisdom and the short duration that you have known me for. I am open to any misgivings from you now and ever after.

'Do not please, by any means, consider this as me pressurizing you. You have time and your freedom to confabulate, and I urge that you include Ruby in the rounds of consultation in case she has second thoughts—though I dread things going awry, especially pertaining to Ruby's decision. Believing in the absence of any infirmity in her love, I leave the rest to the will of God and request you to be kind in your judgement. I know judgement, by its nature, is cold and harsh, not toned down by sympathy or sentiment.

'Let me also inform you that I will be leaving for my journey home on the 13th of September. I couldn't have gone without my effort to resolve matters and be undisturbed to face my parents at home. It may seem that I'm making free with your tolerance and presuming too much. Perhaps my closeness to Ruby is at the back of what may seem my reaching, for which I apologize. More pressing is the very little time before I board the train for my journey.'

The wedding of Ruby and Vikram was a beautiful ceremony held at the quaint and charming St. Mary's Church. The church was surrounded by lush greenery and tall trees that added to the serene ambience of the place. The air was filled with the sweet fragrance of blooming flowers that adorned the church gardens. The church was a magnificent piece of architecture with its tall spires and intricate stained-glass windows that filtered the warm rays of the sun, thereby creating a mesmerizing effect.

As the ceremony began, Ruby, looking radiant in her white gown, walked down the aisle with her father as Alva, her mother, stood with the priest. Vikram waited at the altar, looking handsome in his black suit and tie. Their relatives and friends filled the pews, beaming with happiness and excitement.

The ceremony proceeded with the exchange of vows, rings and the holy sacrament of marriage. The priest's voice echoed in the hall, and the choir sang melodious hymns that filled the hearts of everyone present with joy and love. The couple kissed each other to seal their love.

As the ceremony drew to a close, a strain of sadness filled Ruby's heart, knowing she couldn't go with Vikram to Bandepur. She had to stay back. However, she put on a brave face.

The word 'journey', uttered so casually, cast an instant spell of silence on them all. Unheard, it echoed differently in the chambers of their mind.

Father Constantine found himself lost; his straggler soul, seeking the right path in his tortuous journey to salvation, like a stray lamb seeking to be led by the good shepherd into the shed of the chosen. Alva was anxious about Vikram's packing. She was not quite sure about the ability of her daughter to take care of the nitty-gritty of a man's baggage. She was afraid Ruby might make a mess of things and wouldn't know what all of the linen shall go into the big suitcase and what, besides his shaving things, into the handbag; she was going to handle a situation like this on her own for the first time. Alva worked herself into a frenzy and ended up, hands down, thinking that she couldn't be everywhere and couldn't get things done the way she thought the best way, her way. And then, soon enough, she began to wonder why she was getting so involved. Because of her daughter, she must learn to leave her affairs to the girl, not push into her shoes and fret. Ruby was grown up enough to take care of her life, and now she had an intelligent man like Vikram by her side to be of support in any situation.

For Ruby, the 'journey' sounded like the stark reality of her separation from her dear Vikram, and she didn't know, she wasn't quite certain, for how long. The uncertainty of the period that she was going to be away from him worried her. Vikram had, a thousand times, assured her that it wouldn't be much more than a fortnight. Her mind, nevertheless, was filled with dark apprehensions. They seemed to choke her. Even the slightest expression of the apprehensions that seemed to possess her, in word or gesture, her scepticism, would mean her distrust of her loving husband, and so soon after the solemnizing of the ceremony. It was as if her father had officiated their wedding only yesterday with tears of happiness in his eyes. Leaving all that was yet to unfold with time, as and when it was opportune, she gave herself up to the chores at hand.

Formidable and most challenging for Vikram, the 'journey' was a complex number of things put together. It was an awful prospect to be separated from Ruby, knowing how she was going to suffer in her solitary state, even though surrounded by family and friends at her place of work and in the neighbourhood; how would she bear the loneliness of her heart! She was devoted to her duties at the hospital, but at home and even during her time at the club, she would still be alone. There's no one he could think of, anyone with whom she could share even a bit of her personal matter. With her mother, she could, at best, talk only by indirection to foment the sore inside.

8

Over the days, as the distance from Ruby increased, and Vikram's train brought him closer to Ambala from Amritsar, which it had left behind around three hours back, his mind shot forth and began hovering around the precincts of Bandepur and the town of Sonepat where he had grown up. His mind returned to the friends of his adolescence, especially Kailash, the bookshop owner, Madhusudan, who was called by his female friends and admirers (as he was, indeed, a fair and handsome fellow) just 'Hon' (short for 'honey,' the English for 'Madhu') and Balkrishna. He recalled the times he spent in their company.

The warmth of the swarming memories moved him with a quaver, and he wondered. Yet the images seemed to have lost a shade of their first possessive magic. Other matters had taken possession of him with, but not a very thick cloud cover. He looked forward to spending time with his friends if only to level the remains of the tensions from those tumult of events.

Above all, he thought of his father, Kesar Prasad, the stern lines of his face that daunted everyone else but grew mild and smiling with fond affection when he saw his very own Vikram.

Vikram was slightly jittery this time to face him. His train advanced towards his destination with contrary emotions of nostalgia and apprehension churning in his breast. He knew that he would be swimming against the current when he faced his father with the confession he had to make. He had come and decided to face all the consequences of all that he had kept to himself until now. Ruby's parents had stood by him all through and had performed the solemn Christian marriage ceremony quite willingly. He had never felt even a faint compunction all through; all that he did was in good faith. On the contrary, he felt easy in his conscience because he had no sly designs; therefore, he was prepared to face his people at home uninhibited.

Now though, as he closed in on his hometown, he began to feel a sense of guilt gathering over all other emotions for not having shared something of such importance in his life with his father and the rest of his family. But within himself, he felt quite above board; he thought he should be able to bring his father around to accept and endorse the inevitability of what he was led into doing under compelling circumstances, which he didn't have anyone else to blame for, and which was now almost irrevocable.

He was also weighed down with added contrition of having kept his parents in the dark of his goings-on in Gujarat, where they had sent him with such great trust that he would hold the family honour high and untainted. (Of course, a heap of misdoings stank since his clandestine forays into the sleazy side of life when he was a student in London.) Suddenly, misgivings seemed to be crowding and stampeding him. All that at one time seemed so simple and forthright, with which he could face his father, Shriyut Kesar Prasad, the Mayor of Sonepat. But, as the prospect of coming to face him drew nearer and presented itself as a looming and tangible reality, there appeared something of an ominously dark and overwhelming pall about it, about which there was neither anything simple nor forthright. It metamorphosed into a winding labyrinth, enveloped in a dark miasmic cloud. Yet, a core of truth lay in what he was preparing to say to his father; that was armour for protection, which steadied and emboldened him. And it was all in the realm of his imagination like Quixote brandishing his sword at windmills.

In the mellowed light of the declining sun, he awoke to the constant rumble of wheels. The fields and villages were alive and stirring with human life, whirling by, with signs of the approaching city where his awesome journey was to end.

Kesar Prasad had arrived at the railway station almost an hour before the train's arrival, at a quarter after five, despite the hot afternoon sun. Of course, earlier in the day, he had given instructions to his coachman, Ramawtar, to ready their tonga to go to the station later in the afternoon. Agog with emotion at the prospect of seeing his son, he remained oblivious to the heat of the day as well as the zealous sloganeering procession going on upon a distant road, past the post office in the town; he ignored the more than usual number of people on the platform wearing white Gandhi caps, scurrying about importantly.

Vikram witnessed the Quit India movement in full swing. The streets were filled with supporters of Gandhi's non-violent movement, shouting slogans and sweating under the hot sun. The police, dressed in smart uniforms, patrolled the area with batons and long staffs, trying to maintain some semblance of law and order.

Newspapers were filled with headlines about the movement, and it was evident that it had gained significant support across various towns and cities in India. Vikram was drawn to the cause and joined the movement, dedicating himself to the fight for India's independence.

The government responded with force as the movement gained momentum, leading to widespread arrests and violence. Despite this, the movement continued to grow, and Vikram actively organised protests and spread awareness about the cause.

The Quit India Movement proved pivotal in India's struggle for independence, ultimately leading to the country's liberation from British rule. Vikram's participation in the movement played a small but significant role in this historic event.

The train began to roll into the tin-roofed platform of the station. Even here, there were posters depicting the iconic figure of Gandhi with his long staff, in a long stride, followed by a winding river of a thousand followers in his wake—his legend in big and black handwritten letters. 'Quit India' was pasted on to any convenient place, either around a pillar or on the tea vendor's wheelbarrow. Some railway staff had been specially deployed to peel off the posters, which had been pasted surreptitiously overnight, as much and as many as possible. In the streets and empty lots of the town, the processions terminated and turned into a loud gathering to be addressed by some second-generation leader, a constant reminder to the ruling power that the time to redeem their word of handing over power to India after the end of the Second World War was here.

Leaning out of his coupe's window, Vikram could spot his father's tall figure, as he, dodging the crowd, walked alongside the train that was slowing down. With a protracted screech of brakes, it came to a stop. Vikram leaned far out and, as soon as his father was within sight, he flung an arm out and waved. Already looking out more eagerly as the first- and second-class compartments began to pass by, the observant Kesar Prasad waved back, a broad smile on his face when he noticed his son waving. Everyone tried to beat the next in that jostling crowd at the carriage gates, and in an effort to overtake others to alight, they brought their hand baggage with them. Their endeavours, with numerous packages, worsened the condition and choked the exit.

Ramawtar squeezed into the compartment from another entrance less crowded to get Vikram's luggage out. As the crowd disgorged from the exit Vikram, too, drifted out of the compartment almost straight into his father's arms on the platform. He remained there for a long moment, blissful for both of them and into his father's ear, he whispered, 'O, I'm happy to be home, Papa. How's mama darling?' and left it that. Kesar Prasad saw Ramawtar coming, winding his way through the crowd to them with the baggage. He disengaged and, holding Vikram by his hand, with a slight tug, began walking, erect and brisk, towards the platform exit. He moved his arm around his son's shoulders, and behind him followed Ramawtar, trying to keep pace with his master. Kesar Prasad continued to have a contented smile on his face. Agog with emotion, he just stuttered, 'Come, come,' and walked straight to their waiting tonga through the exit, a wicket gate outside the platform. Vikram quickly bought a bunch of bananas from a fruit wheelbarrow outside the station and, with an affectionate pat on the horse's neck, he fed him the bananas. He lent the support of his hand to his father for him to climb up the back seat, after which he almost hopped up with his foot on the footrest to sit by his father's side.

Ramawtar had shoved the pieces of luggage deep under the seat, and there was enough space to sit without cramping their legs. The pleated seat covers were a pink and grey floral print hanging over their seats to conceal the luggage. It also gave their conveyance the appearance of personally-owned transport, distinct from the commercial ones that were covered with uniformly coloured plastic sheets.

The familiar scents and sights of the bazaars through which they passed gave Vikram the feeling that truly brought him back home. The rows of shops lining the road were bustling with business—hardware, building materials, crockery, household electric and other mechanical appliances; cloth merchants were selling fabrics of all kinds and colours and ready-made garments displayed on hangers on shop fronts. The shopkeepers were busy dealing with the bargaining, garrulous customers. The most tempting smells emanated to fill Vikram with nostalgia from the halwai shops where huge globular puris were being fried to go with the potato curry made with an oriental blend of spices. The scent wafted and filled the street air, and his mouth filled with saliva at the thought of it being served with a dash of mango pickle. He found himself plunged back—carefree into the streets with a friend or two on their bicycles, snaking through the shoppers with their blown bags. O, what larks! It indeed was a time of their life when everything else was taken care of by their parents, and there had not been a vexing flea to worry about.

He began to wonder if he would be able to find some of his friends from the old school days there; maybe they could sit in a coffee house and pull yarn for hours on end as before.

Shoving the memories back into the mind where they belonged, he found the tonga pulling up in front of the entrance to their sprawling house on its lawn. A gravel path ran up to the porch of the two-step entry into the house, and there was a playground at the rear. At the door, they were met by Vikram's mother, who had been waiting to have her son in her arms. She brushed away a tear or two of joy and smothered the rising sob on seeing her son in person and hugging him. Beside her was Bindia, the all-round domestic help and the wife of Ramawtar. Ramawtar also looked after the mowing of grass and furrows and the pots of flowers on the veranda. Vikram said he'd have a warm bath after a cup of tea, which had already been prepared by Bindia and kept ready for the family.

After tea, it would be rather late to go out, he thought. Vikram's father, too, advised him against it. He suggested he give himself a good long night's rest and sleep off the fatigue of the journey. He knew Vikram was keen to go out and see his friends.

Abandoning his plans for the next day, Vikram spent some time of the rest of the evening chatting with his parents and playing with nine-year-old Raghav, his sister's son who was at his naani's, visiting for a few days.

He recounted to his mother the travails of eating out until he found Mastram and the team to set up his kitchen and take care of his house and the small lawn, both allotted to him by the Punjab state government, and how he missed the smells and taste of his mother's cooking. And then, how bored he had been with his lonesome hours of prolonged evenings and how he had decided to join the only decent club in town. His doctor friend was already a member, who initiated him and gave him company most of the evenings. He all but stopped short of going over the episode of his meeting with Ruby.

He told his little nephew the funny tale of a cross-eyed shopkeeper who turned his face awry when a customer came in and began attending to him. Some hid their smile when they found him talking to someone imaginary a little on the side from the real customer, who stood right in front of him. Their amusement and laughter livened up the atmosphere. In the middle of it all, Vikram yawned, then yawned again after a little while, and it glistened in his eyes. Sleep seemed to be fast overpowering him.

'Your bed is made, Vicky. You go and rest if you feel like it. If you wish to retire for the night early—you must be tired after the long journey. I'll tell Bindia to serve you an early dinner. She's done with her cooking.'

'Yes, Mama, that is a great idea. Only a mom like you can come up with an idea that is best for her child. I'd rather eat and get into my bed. Father, as usual, will keep you company at dinner. I'm sure he as ever keeps his time.'

Kusum, his mother, laughed softly and said, 'O yes, and still gets cheesed off if there's a visitor or an intruder. Come to the table, but wash your hands first.' And she smiled, seeing that Vikram was smiling; he walked up to the wash basin and obediently washed his hands. For a moment, he felt like he was eight and not thirty. Time does play tricks, but the human mind, he thought, was resilient enough as a web to take in all its swings.

Vikram woke up, his mind crowded with memories of Ruby in their newly set-up Gujarat home. Deciding within himself to find enough time during the afternoon to write and give his darling girl the summary of his day, whatever would give Ruby a wholesome idea of his life since he had left her in Gujarat a few days back. But the bright sun sharply defined the Bandepur ambience and perked his desire to go out cycling on his squeaky bicycle. He wished to seek adventure in the fresh country breeze, like in the good old days; to again meet up with school friends. And so, after a quick breakfast of puri and halwa specially made for him by his mother, he strode out into the fresh morning air. Yet, he turned a bit pensive as thoughts of Ruby once again rose like a bubble in his mind as he walked towards his cycle leaning on its stand, spick after being cleaned and oiled, as he liked it. He caught a fleeting sight of Bindia in the kitchen window, following him with her smiling eyes.

He climbed onto the bicycle seat, and it didn't take him long to start pedalling his way, whirring across the gravel path out of the gate.

He was headed on the road to Sonepat, full of nostalgia for sights and smells embedded in his memory of familiar pockmarked streets. But as he let his sight move across gradually, he noticed new houses and gleaming shops with glazed windows come up, and without many of the old landmarks left, it didn't seem as familiar. He fondly remembered and thought of Kailash, Balkrishna and Madhusudan. From the outskirts, as he turned into the township, he hit the Jail Road off the old site of the district courts that led into the heart of the town. At the very turn into Harnamdas Lane was Madhusudan's house. An electric engineer employed in the Department of Electricity of the Ministry of Power in the state, he had been allotted one of the prized official residences. Vikram followed the indication and decided to look in to see if Madhu was at home. He had written to all of them about a week before he left Gujarat. This morning he couldn't call anyone, for he was not quite sure what time he would be able to start out.

Madhu's mother met Vicky with élan and wouldn't allow him to leave without having tea and snacks. A neighbour had, a few days back, returned from a pilgrimage to Mathura (the ground of Krishna's childhood romps with other boys and girls his age) located alongside the Yamuna, and brought prasad (part of the offering at the altar of the deity) of pedas, which she said Vicky and Madhu must have before she would allow them to go out. Pedas are cherished by those who know the quality of the sweet milk product with the stamp of Mathura on it. These, in addition, were sacrosanct, presented as an offering to the Lord. They ate their pedas, and in a hurry to be together, quickly said 'bye' to Bhatia Aunty and rode off on their bikes.

Soon after, they turned towards East Avenue, heading to the 'Trio Cafe' as usual; of course, on their way, they decided to see if they could get Kailash also. His brother Dado normally took care of the bookshop during the middle of the day. Dado came to the shop after lunch, around noon. Kailash could take time off between noon and seven in the evening, the closing time for the market. They didn't find Kailash in the shop, and Dado was sitting slightly morose in his open cubicle just inside the glass door. His typical frown brought out thin vertical folds of pimpled skin to the middle of his brows; his smile, though, was babyish and innocent. From Dado, they came to know that Kailash had been called back home early to take their mother to King Edward Hospital, where he knew a senior doctor, Guy Mitchell.

Sometime in the middle of the night, she had developed an intestinal disorder because of a late and rather spicy dinner she'd had at a party in the neighbourhood; she had passed loose stools several times and had a few bouts of vomiting. As it was an emergency, she was taken straight to the hospital's intensive care unit. 'He is still with her in the hospital. But as our mother's condition is under control, he should be back in about an hour,' Dado told them. For some moments, they were undecided about whether or not to go to the hospital. But considering everything, the intrusion, they thought, would be improper. With a heavy heart, they said a few words of cheer to Dado and left.

The mild autumn sun made it lovely to go cycling, especially with chums. They wound their way through the sparse shopping crowd in the Avenue, directly moving to the Trio.

Then out of the blue, Madhusudan observed, 'Looking at the movement of life around, quite impervious to graver things waiting on the horizon to assault us, anyone would gather that it is all hunky-dory and that life goes on as ever at an even keel. The pity, Vicky, is the general unawareness or sheer political indifference, which, of course, cannot continue in the face of the beastly and fierce tornado brewing in India. Not with the strategic mind of wartime British Prime Minister Winston Churchill, scheming thousands of miles across the globe. Constrained to freeing the colony, they took discreet gradual measures. It must have been a painful decision, for the gleanings from this colony has padded the empire's coffers and turned London into the epicentre of world trade. And so, he is going to withdraw, leaving in his wake a situation that both sides, led by Jinnah and Nehru, would likely for a long time have a lot on their plates to grapple with, enough to rue the gruelling confrontations they had skirmished through to freedom. And engaged with the ascendance of their muscular strength for the ongoing squabbles and skirmishes, the welfare of the masses, the time of peace to build their schools, hospitals and research laboratories—the efforts to be in step with the advancing world of science and technology, will get dumped.'

They were closing in on their destination, but Madhusudan continued in great passion, haranguing on what he knew about the politically developing situation dangerously advancing towards the feared and undesirable partition of the country, especially on religious grounds. 'Now, convinced by the situation on the ground in the country, the Muslim separatist stand following the line of the two-nation theory, propounded and delineated in the hardliner Choudhry Rahmat Ali's pamphlet, *Now or Never* in 1933, had especially hardened. By 1940, Lord Linlithgow decided that it was time that the British government partly devolve power to the local leaders to deal with the developing prickly communal conditions, and he was ready to support the grant of Dominion status to India. Next thing we know, Sir Stafford Cripps had arrived in our country in 1942 with his proposal from the London British Colonial Office of granting Dominion status to India (what later came to be known as the Cripps Mission).

'There was no end to the apprehensions of certain sections of Muslims. In contrast, certain eminent Muslim leaders, too, had joined the Indian National Congress and were working side by side with Hindu leaders for the freedom of the country. The prevalent idea, even among some eminent Muslim leaders, is that India would remain unified even if the Muslim demand for a homeland was realised. Jinnah strongly supported Choudhry Rahmat Ali's two-nation theory. He considered the communities of Hindus and Muslims as "two irreconcilable monoliths". Considering the Turkish attitude of high-handedness shown towards Islamic pockets of possession in the Middle East, and Muslim misgivings ensuing from the hostile attitude of the British towards Turkey, a supporter of the Allies in the Second World War, the Muslims in India, chary of the policies of the English colonial government, have rejected the proposal. The rejection came in spite of British assurance, in the form of the addition of a clause in the Dominion status document, that no province or princely state, whether Hindu or Muslim, would be forced to join the Dominion of India.'

Both of them, Vikram and Madhusudan, levered up the brakes as they reached the entrance of the Trio and quickly found parking spots for their bikes. They walked up the few steps leading to the double glass doors of the entrance. Madhusudan led the way, and they walked through the main hall to the door opening on the north side and onto the grassy patio, where some tables were laid, a few of which were occupied. They were lucky to locate an unoccupied table on the edge, under a poplar, the kind Vicky would prefer any day. He fancied sitting under the tree with patches of sun and shade moving along the foliage, waving in the soft breeze. There was also enough shade to avoid coming in contact with bird droppings.

'Two coffees, hot and strong, and a plate of vadas with

no sambhar—only the staple white chutney to go with the vadas,' Madhusudan turned and told the waiter who had come and stood deferentially by their table. He had placed a tray with a few tumblers of water on it. He didn't need to consult Vikram regarding their order; he knew his friend's preferences. They settled down, sipping their steaming coffee and savouring the flavour of fresh and crisp vadas.

Vikram was fully aware of the developments in the sociopolitical situation in the country and understandably better informed. Triggered by what his friend had remarked, his mind was engaged with the recent history of British India, especially since the abrupt end of the war following the nuclear attack. The flavour of the coffee and vadas, he felt, was tempered by stifling thoughts of the ruthlessly repressive attitude of the kid-gloved hands of the rulers. He quickly gulped down the last dregs of his coffee and said, 'You are right, Madhu. But to my mind, there's much more than what meets the eye. Since the time that Choudhry Rahmat Ali's pamphlet set afloat the idea of a two-nation theory, which was tabled by the Muslim Delegation in the Parliamentary Reforms Committee and rejected, the "apprehensive" mind of the Muslims in India, as you put it, has been restless about the community being a minority, and for no particularly apparent reason, they continue to dog their apprehensions with a vague fear of being dominated by the majority Hindu community of the country. In spite of periodic and perfunctory steps that the British government have taken to assure the Muslim community that their interests are being taken care of, their apprehensive fears are not allayed. Therefore, politically conscious minorities have come together under ambitious leaders seeking the limelight, and political parties have begun to take shape. The interesting part, Madhu, is that they are successful as good politicians of modern times.

'Majorly among them are—under the leadership of Fazlul Huq, the Krishak Praja Party in Bengal. There is another, the "Unionist Party", under the leadership of Sikandar Hayat Khan in Punjab, who later mustered the help of Congress and the newly conceived Shiromani Akali Dal to form a viable government in the Province of Punjab. The Unionists were a splinter group of the mainstream Muslim League and held on to the view that, though the Muslims were a minority and should be shown special consideration and given a reservation of seats in the House of Representatives in the state and the centre—from constituencies with a concentrated Muslim population—they'd prefer to remain a part of a united India. They later formed a united government with the support of Congress and the Shiromani Akali Dal. The polarization of communities and groups under separate political party flags has created cracks in the formidable monolith of the growing voters' list. This was clearly reflected in the number of seats won by the communities in pockets of high concentration by the results of the general elections of 1945 and the Provincial elections in 1946. The polity has been weakened by division, and this is easier for the British rulers to handle. There were unbending hardliners in every group and sub-group, who, at the same time, were power hungry and aided the cause of the rulers.'

As he pushed his emptied cup away, almost like a reflex action, heaving a sigh of relief, he looked at Madhu with a broad smile and said, 'I'm going to have another coffee, Madhu; what about you? Oh yes, I'm sure you'd like something to brush off the boredom brought on by this harangue on our recent turbulent history. But it's good to be aware after Nehru's angry outburst during his press conference on July 10, only a year ago. It was like throwing the whole book into the face of the Cabinet Mission led by Lord Pethick-Lawrence and Stafford Cripps. Besides, more importantly, my dear Madhu, Nehru could foresee that the proposed groupings and the proposed number of cabinet seats shared by the Congress and the Muslim League in the Interim Government at the Centre would make it too precariously balanced to hold together long enough and run the government. This blew all prospects of settlement between Muslims and Hindus. You can call it a balancing act by the departing British; some thought it was the shrewd British political strategy of divide and rule. To cap it all, there followed, in the name of Direct Action, the great Calcutta killings. This was initiated and encouraged by Suhrawardy, the Chief Minister of Bengal, after his address to the Muslim crowd, proclaiming the demand for a Muslim homeland, 'Pakistan', under the two-nation theory. Of this, Muhammad Ali Jinnah was a strong supporter. The crowd returning from the Suhrawardy rally turned violent and there ensued large-scale ruthless carnage. The aroused Hindus retaliated and, in the communal riots, casualties ran up to five thousand. Consequently, the partition of the country, in spite of Gandhi's strong moral force of effort at resistance, reflected in his fast unto death, is now ominously looming as inevitable.'

Madhusudan told the waiter at their table to make it not one, but two coffees, again hot and strong, but no more snacks, for they were being awaited back home for lunch. Vicky had told his mother before he left that for lunch, he would like to gorge on the shahi paneer prepared by her deft hands, as he had since boyhood loved the dish. It had been such a while since he'd tasted it. Though being with friends, he may get late, he was sure enough that he'd return to eat with her.

But Vikram was so possessed by the subject that was going to decide the future of the country that, before the waiter brought in their second round of coffee, he picked up the loose end and continued. 'Sparked in Bengal, the communal violence has spread like a forest fire to Bihar, and has proven Sardar Patel correct in his observation about the Muslim population and its allegiance to the idea of the Muslim homeland of Pakistan. Violence flared up in Punjab and Sind provinces, too, especially in the districts where the Muslim population abounded. My heart is truly heavy with apprehensions especially given that even the Congress is not prepared to go the way shown by the wisdom of Gandhi. Now, we can only timorously wait for the seal to be put on the papers and prepare to face the consequences. It is an awful thought.'

How awful were the events that came in the wake of the carving of a nation from mainland India! No one could have foreseen; still, the first blood drawn in Suhrawardy's Calcutta hadn't fully dried.

Vikram landed back home almost an hour too late for lunch and saw his mother with a mild frown, looking at her wristwatch. She was still waiting for him to have lunch together. His father, though, had eaten and gone for his usual hour's siesta before he went back to his business.

After a while; he woke up from his rather longish afternoon postprandial snooze. Enmeshed in the thoughts of Ruby as he looked at his watch, he found it was after half past five, and he badly wanted his evening cup of tea to shake off the general fatigue and laziness. His mother told him to come to the table for his tea and told him that his father wanted to talk to him when he returned from the office at about half past six. Mentally, he began to brace up for the forthcoming encounter with his father, which he knew had to come sooner or later; but sooner, the better, he thought. He, too, had his mind made up to come clean and get the weight off his chest. Get it over with at the earliest and atone for his lapse of not having kept his father in the loop about his life away from home. He had nothing to hide; only perhaps, adding to what he had gathered from his sources. To give his father the bare truth of all that he had gone through and out of discomfiting timorousness. His tender emotional bond with Ruby was growing stronger by the day, and he hadn't shared it with his father when he should have. He, therefore, desired to shake off the burden that he seemed to carry. He believed that truth had just one version, once and for all. True, of course, that if there were any blanks in his narrative, the experience and wisdom of his father would provide the fillers without distortion and save him embarrassment.

So, as the hands of the wall clock closed on seven, he walked up to his father's room, sure that he was through with his refreshing repast.

The apprehension of a showdown caused some trepidation in him but without moist or trembling hands. Aware of his father's affection for him and his very reasonable temperament, his concern wasn't of any formidable magnitude. And by the time he entered his father's room, the missing beats of his heart were under his full control. More so, because in spite of his father being in the process of twirling his moustache, he had his best genial smile to welcome his dear son as he entered the room.

His father knew that Kusum could as well handle, perhaps in certain ways better than he would, the situation arising from what Vikram's reaction would be to the kind of decision they, in his absence, had taken on his behalf.

The feeling of guilt would have borne down heavily on Kusum. They had deprived their son of any say, leaving aside his prerogative, in the most vital matter related to his life. It was especially important in the case of a person like Vikram, their son, whom they knew, in spite of his affection and obedience to them as parents, always had held independent views when it came to matters so intimately personal to have a bearing on his entire life. Therefore, the decision had been to let Kesar Prasad handle the talk, for he could adequately cut out the emotional part from the discussion between two grown, intelligent men.

Kesar Prasad got up from his chair when he saw Vikram softly opening the door and walking in. Vikram smiled as he met his father's eye, and wasn't he truly happy? The father put his affectionate arm around his son's shoulder and led him to the other chair that he had arranged for him, close to where he sat.

'I'm sure you've heard that judge announcing in his court with a few significant implications: The court was not born yesterday and to have chiefly caused amusement among his audience, which was included in his intentions.' And so saying, he too laughed a little. A bit baffled, Vikram was, in a flash, close enough to catch on with the indirection of his father's statement. But the time to react would come only after his father clarified what he wanted to say to his son. And, therefore, noticing a small smile on his son's face, Kesar Prasad continued, 'I am happy to see you have sense, faith and patience to hold on until I am through with what I have to say to you. And indeed, I will not mince my words, especially with an intelligent young man like you, a barrister.

'Through my own source of information, I have learnt about the affair you were having with that Christian girl, Ruby, her name, isn't it? And because the affair is immature—I mean, going by the experience of your young age, it is quite natural to happen—but was shaping up to engage you more than casually, this friend of the family, my source, thought and was candid with me. He said, "Not a happy sign for the fair name of the family." And also, in consideration of your official status and reputation, he showed his urgency in telephoning me on a long-distance call. He gave me his version of the information. And, let me assure you, without getting into any ado, that I decided to share it with your mother. I did. More down to earth than I, she pondered over the matter for a couple of days; then she broke the matter with her mother; she told me later.

'You know how your Pushpa Nani dotes on you and must deal with the apprehension of you falling into some trap. It caused a flutter in the ladies' quarters. They were in a hurry to decide upon the matter. I failed to warn them not to allow their concern to precipitate the matter this way or that without talking things over with you. The undesirable happened. Letting you know about the developing circumstances and discussing it with you—after all, it is a decision that was going to settle the course and quality of life for you—had never crossed their mind. I never got to talk intimately with them. Together, as elders to their young wayward ward, in their wisdom, in sync with accepted and approved established moral and ethical wisdom to give shape and direction to your life, they, your mother with her mother's greater experience of life, came to a conclusion, which you may consider an open question. And, therefore, too, you may consider the idea an inconsequential and pedestrian thing, but the best thing for the young, who begin to show signs of straying away, led by the siren-charm of wanton women from brick-laid streets of the fish market, is to get them anchored in wedlock—the age-old panacea for those who pursue dreams.

'They didn't just stop there. The family purohita, Omkarnath after finalising a round of confabulations was promptly and expressly sent to the Sunehri Haveli of the Sharmas in Baiyanpur with a properly worded message. The message could neither be taken lightly for the added reason of it having come from the house of Ranas of Bandepur nor could it be interpreted as a non-negotiable commitment. It was polite and correct, both in language and delivery. The relevant part is that it has been accepted, and everything has been decided. We have neither broached the subject of dowry nor, of course, did they mention it but, rest assured, I'm fully aware that maybe injustice is being done to you, as seen from your standpoint. I do really wish that they had kept you in the loop, and waited for you to not only bring you up to date with whatever was being decided on your behalf but also taken your opinion into consideration before coming to any conclusion of their cogitation or pitching into a decision. This is more like being imposed upon, which even a schoolboy would resent.

'Besides, talking face to face does make a great deal of difference. For the bare rational approach to eliminate contention has to gain strength and support from a human element. Its efficacy mounts manifold, that is when his own well-wishing kin is present. All argument takes place in their presence, including his own. These would largely be the ideals that you would easily identify with, but taking into account that man, by the native element, is born to look for ideals, though they, like moonbeams, slip to leave the palm dark when to grasp he encloses round them. Reality is gross and flawed, and it stuns us by its difference from the image in the mind. Yet, even with some compromise, the inexorable reality has to be said yes to.

'You know, Vikram, only when a sense of guilt possesses a man, he tends to use too many words. More eager than you are in wanting to tell me your version of what actually transpired, what authentically is the ground reality, I am impatient to learn how much and where I have erred, in spite of my filial intention of being your total well-wisher. And then I've exposed my tender and not a little tarnished underbelly. There is already a confession of guilt present here, and still, let my acquiescence be presumed to something evidently unfair. One last thing I'd like to add here is that the communications between the families are no mere parleys. We are two very respectable families of the area, cordially disposed to each other, though actual interaction may have been infrequent. Furthermore, the current exchanges have been towards a decision that, I'm sure you can appreciate, is mutually understood and almost sacrosanct for both families. It is the word of a gentleman.'

Vikram sat across from his father, feeling the familiar warmth of home, and began with a start. 'Believe me, father,' he said. 'Just being here with you and hearing your kind words, I feel like I'm back where I belong. Even though we might have had a difficult conversation, I still feel your love surrounding me.'

His father smiled, 'I'm glad to hear that, my son. I wanted to talk to you about something important, and I'm relieved that you understand where I'm coming from.'

Vikram nodded, 'Yes, you explained everything so well that I don't have any questions. But now that I'm aware of the situation, I feel guilty for not keeping you informed of what was happening in my life. I should have told you more about what I was up to.'

His father put a hand on Vikram's shoulder, 'Don't beat yourself up, son. What's done is done. Just focus on moving forward and keeping an open line of communication between us. That's all I ask.'

Vikram nodded again, 'You're right, Father. I'll make sure to keep you updated from now on. Thank you for your understanding and love.

'The source, our trusted friend, who revealed the information of my familiarity with the Christian girl, was largely correct. But you can understand that it was a matter of a relationship between two human beings—the beginnings and a period of nascence were naturally delicate and tentative and surreptitious as such, and your source couldn't have been exact in every detail. Looking back not too far, even I now consider it rather full of complications, twists and turns. To shadow or show an unusual interest in peeking into others' life could have exposed him to an infamous scandal. I appreciate his caution of "thus far and no farther".

'But it is time for my reckoning. Barring private shame, I am going to be absolutely truthful about what I mentioned as the "factual details" of what has happened over a period of more than a year. I am your son, and I've within me enough strong moral fibre to face up to and own my lapses, even though they may be of personal shameful slip-ups. From the moment I met Ruby in the club—yes, she is the daughter of a Christian clergyman—I became conscious of her candid eyes through which peeps a rare trustworthiness. I was impressed by more things than one about her, or else...perhaps I would have terminated the encounter forthwith.

'She sat there and talked of several common things of interest and also, for no particular reason, her attachment to her family. And indeed, her demure conduct reflected her culture and her rearing. What with another round of drinks and a couple of dances with her, she got rather late, much later than usual, when she took an occasional detour via the club on her way back home from the hospital. So, to set her parents' minds at rest, I offered to see her home in my car. I did so. And while I was there at their doorstep, her mother appeared in the light of the open door. When she saw her daughter had come home in the company of a stranger, she asked me to come in. Soon after Father Constantine joined us. I did the explaining as best as I could. Politely took upon myself the responsibility of having kept them waiting for their daughter into the night. It was almost eleven. I appropriately introduced myself to them, bowed apologetically and took my leave of them.

'From then on, whatever little time I could find in my busy schedule at my office in the courts, and whatever time Ruby spent in my company, was with the knowledge and consent of her parents. I told her always truthfully to keep her parents informed that she was seeing me. We sometimes did, but rather rarely, go to see a movie if there was a good one, like *Ben Hur* or *Cleopatra,* at one of the two cinema theatres in the town. And whenever her schedule was upset by our going out to eat or just going out of town for a drive towards the small lake—hidden within a huge mango orchard about three or four miles from the central town of Gujarat—I always went to see her back home. I'm sure you can understand that some intimacy did develop between us, and also that I was careful and cautious not to transgress decency.

'Until one day, perhaps under the mounting pressure of social constraints and apprehension of wild canards, she asked me if she could come to my rooms to see me, rather than in the club or out in public, which left her very self-conscious. Her nerves were taut. Most people from her nursing job at Ford's Hospital recognised her and perhaps gave her a look upon seeing her in a man's company. And indeed, it took me by surprise. But at the same time, I was glad to notice how untainted and free her mind was from an inhibitive or apprehensive sense caused by a secret design. Considering her conduct positively, I came to see it as the faith she showed in me, which was remarkable. And therefore, it took me not much time to tell her that she was free to come over. She knew the hours that I would be at home and when I would not be. And I told her I'd instruct the servants to take care if she had to wait in my absence.

'As I now see it, it must have been during this period when she began to visit me at my apartment that your friend must have felt alarmed and wrote to you about how the matter was turning serious and required the intervention of the elders and suggested wise and urgent action. From his surveillance, he must have concluded that the girl's visits were more frequent than could be overlooked. Consequent upon which, all my revered well-wishers hastily planned and ensued this present irrevocable situation. But my story remains only half told. And now, I seem to have come to the darkest part of the alley, which ends in a dead end. A wall.

This darkness, Father, I believe is a sort of conglomerate of my guilt of things past, not just my goings on and not having shared with you how seriously I was getting involved in my relationship with Ruby; the guilt of taking many things for granted, only because the developments were happening in almost full knowledge of the Constantine family; and so were sanctified, and I presumed that the same would hold true for you and the family. Once again, I was blind to the reality of the identities of individuals comprising the family. I thought the whole bunch was embodied in you, though even that was a blind spot I didn't care to consider.

'No wonder, therefore, I find myself groping in the dark. Besides the darkness of the blind spot, there's this helplessness in the face of this ongoing admission that I have to make. And so, with the backing of the tacit consent of her parents, Ruby's visits tended to be more frequent than even for me to be comfortable with. And to be cautious of such a predicament, I did give her a hint, which I'm afraid she took lightly. In cognizance of my place and status in society, she required maintaining certain standards of propriety, and we were close to flouting them, unheedingly. Perhaps our clear conscience was right, and so was the filial acquiescence; but who was going to rein the wagging tongues in the neighbourhood? Most of all were the full reins that had taken over our elemental human drives and had grown with mutually permissive intimacy.

'So much for my sense of justice. Whatever it was worth, I leave it to your pronouncement—the last word—on it. What weighed most heavily on me was the human element of implicit faith in a chaste loving heart. Beyond this, I do not think there is anything left for me to add. Before the situation, Father, in which your son was the chief personage, became a scandal, I went to Father Constantine and humbly and respectfully asked for his daughter Ruby's hand in marriage. Looking back, dear Father, I know it does seem like a hasty decision. But the ultimate pushing element was a strong and powerful whirlwind of apprehension that this sinister storm may overtake you and the family unawares here and smear you all with spiteful public-created muck. Some diabolic minds do rejoice in the humiliation of the eminent and highly held. The covetous lot!

'I knew I could soon after talk to you about it all. The situation, from my standpoint, quite inadvertently has taken such a turn that I find I am rudderless at sea. I thought and did all I did in good faith to my best understanding. I was driven by my prime concern of saving everyone from ignominy, especially the honour of the girl, who has a simple-hearted faith in my sincerity and was waiting, understandably in great tension, for me to take the next step. At no time did she even hint at marriage. To me, though, tying the knot ceremonially seemed the most honourable solution. I'd never resort to creating a morass of lies around myself, following discomfiture later for one and all. All these and perhaps much more precipitated my decision to call on Ruby's father, Mr Constantine, and mother, Ma'am Alva, with the urgent request to perform the ceremony of marriage between their daughter and me within the aura of sanctity in the church. My intention was to purge it of a stain, if there were any, on our relationship. So was it done—with a minimum of fanfare and the fewest possible guests besides family elders at the post-ceremony luncheon. So that all could be mentally at peace and there would be no room left for public calumniation. To my mind, all that I did in the circumstances was just and within the ambit of propriety; so also for the good of everyone concerned.

'And indeed, I say this without any partiality to myself or my sense of equanimity, and in all humility, I leave it to you for the last word of judgement. You know that this is my truth, and it is fearless; it is candid. Also, dear Father, let me assure you that I shall follow your advice, for I know it is going to be tested on the touchstone of your unbiased wisdom.'

Then Vikram smiled a stunted smile, even present in the middle of a grim situation, as he added, 'It does tend to bend in favour of your favourite Vicky, even in the face of a very complex moral calamity. In the present conundrum, like the one faced by Solomon, I would like your judgement and advice. I cannot, though, cite anything in favour of the Constantines to equal what you said pertinently for the family of the Sharmas of Baiyanpur. I cannot because, truthfully, I am not qualified. But now, Father, you have the facts of the case. You can consider it from any angle. Your acumen needs to examine them before your ripened wisdom derives the conclusion to be followed by my action.'

'I'm proud of you, Vicky, my boy. I'm glad to notice that the balance of mind and control over the strong swing of emotion at your age is remarkable. Yet alas! The pity of it is that the matter, as you put it, is not as simple as that, even if we can keep our sanity. Tell me if I go wrong. To look at it squarely, two things set, one alongside the other, happened at the same time, almost simultaneously, so to say, which has made matters worse. In your place, you were keen on your effort at safeguarding the honour of your family here and Ruby's family there by that single hasty step. On second thought, I believe my letter asking you to come back home soon added urgency to your haste. On the heels of your decision, or perhaps, side by side with your effort, spurred by an eager well-wisher's information, the older ladies, revered for their wisdom, made well-intentioned haste in another direction and advanced to the point of no return. Well-intentioned both, but contrariwise had to clash head-on! And thus, they have been presented to me, duly sugar-coated by your love, to face the music, or shall I say, to face the cacophony of the hullabaloo that may ensue. The situation seems to be readymade material for Hegel's tragedy—good versus right.

'We shall have to sit quietly and ponder a while to straighten the events tangibly inwards to direct our thought. Among the given facts, what stands out is that you have taken an irreversible step, which needs to not only be respected but also protected as a prime guidepost in all further thinking. No less, by any means, is the family's confabulation at my behest, followed by the negotiation. This has brought in an extra factor that cannot be overlooked due to social and moral considerations, which has also led us towards a conclusive decision. Even a slight shift in the weight of loyalties of the two of us, you and I, can create a fatal disaster in the precarious balance in which it now hangs. It is a test of our nerves to stem such a formidable disaster. Taking the challenge head-on is inconceivable. The following disaster would be of a different character but of no less ferocity. In such situations, ancient wise men like Chanakya and Machiavelli suggest a sniper or flank attack instead of a frontal one. The idealist may call it devious, but to my mind, the situation is warlike. And it's not a cliché—all is fair in love and war. The idea flashed across my mind as you were so honestly laying out the facts before me.

'You may think I digress. Yes, I'd resort to digression. I'd like to tell you an untold part, an offshoot of our family history. This secret little section of our family tale the children, you too, inadvertently touched upon in random questions, about your uncle and my brother Badrinath who, with his family, lives in one of the more congested streets downtown and who comes down to visit us only during festivals or family occasions. Kusum does not get along well with that part of the family, not only because she knows quite well about Badrinath being my half-brother. The fact is that his wife, Neelam, is of a temperament incompatible with almost every family member. "Termagant" is the epithet her own sister gave her. That is not all—their children have not been reared or groomed well. They recklessly open and ransack drawers, cabinets and wardrobes as if on a demolishing spree. No wonder Kusum keeps aloof from the family and does not encourage frequent visits. Women are gifted with a special sense of understanding of these subtle undercurrents endlessly going on in the bustle of children's playtime together, or understood during the special lunches and the variety of homemade snacks for the evening tea; after which it is time for the departure of the guest family. On both sides and under their breath, women would mutter, "Oh, good riddance." Yet they both knew that it was only until the next time the inveterate cycle of life in family and society goes on and on, riding roughshod over sharps and flats.

'He is my half-brother because my father and your grandfather happened to marry a second time. I'm sure you must have noticed that your uncle has facial features with a clear indication of being of a mongoloid mould—broad cheekbones, rather compressed and widely placed eyes, and an overhang of slightly swelled upper eyelids that make the eyes look narrower. His mother, and our stepmother, was of Nepalese origin. She had worked a long time as an ayah in the house and therefore, we—my elder sister Deepti and I, as children—learned to call her "Ayah" first, and then more intimately, because of her affection for us, "aunty". Indeed, she was treated like a member of the family by everyone. Then it seems some equations changed, and our father decided to buy a small flat in the town. You're right; it is the same place where Badrinath now resides; Ayah Aunty moved into that small apartment. We all used to go to visit her periodically, although I distinctly remember that our mother went along rather unwillingly. And sometimes, after our father had a tiff with his mother, he disappeared for a few days from home.

'For days sometimes, and mother would fret and grumble

over the occurrence. She'd quietened from her bitter and vexed grumbling and snapping, and I saw that, after some time, she began to take our father's visits to Aunty's apartment in her stride.

'Sometimes later then, we were told, we have a small brother with whom the whole family shall celebrate the next festival of lights, Diwali. Congested as the area was, their apartment had a scant share of sunlight, and it was cold and crowded in there with all their trunks and bedrolls besides the furniture. To me, it really seemed rather cramped. Come Diwali, when we all went there in the family tonga, the air in the rooms was filled with the heavy, luscious and cloying fumes of the sweets being made below in the halwai shops lined along the street. As children, we were more interested in lighting candles and in going to the rooftop to let rockets fly. The crackers shot into the sky and, high up there, sparkled into an expanding globe of multicoloured little stars and then burst into a loud bang of a cracker. Similar jubilations from several other rooftops livened up the whole atmosphere with shouts and laughter. Feeling grubby by the time we began descending down the stairs, the family was winding up their talk about the increase in the number of cars in this small town (since the townsmen bought them from city folk who came to sell off their used cars cheaply) much like their usual exchanges about how the market rates of everything, like onions and tomatoes, were shooting up. And indeed, the ladies and maids were getting bowls of steaming dishes from the kitchen for food to be served in the living room, where some extra chairs had already been brought in.

'Going briefly over this part of our family history, not in the least do I mean to directly or indirectly suggest that since it has happened in the family once, it can be taken as permissive precedent and can happen again. Or that the precedent makes transgression of the norm permissible. If it was a freak, the freak remains to be a freak, a one-off. It does not become an example that may at any time be taken as a beacon of light to be followed or an ideal to be emulated, and so giving way to an aberration to prevail. Personally though, I appreciate and, any day, would be up for upholding the time-confirmed norms of society, would yet, with a buffer, accept what goes by the name of liberalism. In full awareness of all related circumstances, of the better part of which you know best, I leave the decision up to you and your intelligence, my son Vicky, who, as the court said, was not born yesterday and possessed of much knowledge and experience. You will surely take the right decision, weighing all contexts, that I think is the best a man can do in any circumstance. I shall expect, of course, that you share with me your reasons leading you to the decision. I am your father and will always like you to be happy. Ruby is your love and Vidya will add happiness to your life. Let us handle this matter first. We will think about Ruby later.'

'I would like to give myself some time and quiet of disengaged aloofness before I can further continue this conversation, Father. In the meanwhile, it shall give me a break from such a complicated and ponderous issue. I shall have to go over a vast labyrinthine terrain and ponder to come up with an answer. It seems almost impossible to decide upon something that shall be gladly acceptable to all concerned. We all have sharps and flats of our inexorable part of the character, which may leave some with abrasions, and some with lasting injuries. I would not like to be the cause of any deep hurt to anyone, not the least to loved and revered ones. So, Father, I seek your leave to go and see some of my old pals.

'Ah, I've already received two phone calls from Madhusudan since my cup of tea. In fact, I'm going to postpone my outing with them for tomorrow morning. It is rather late now and getting dark. I'll be seeing you, Father,' Vicky said and got up.

He stretched out his stiffened joints and muscles.

Another morning, and it was another day. He woke up with a bright and clear mind, having waded through and leaving behind the bramble bush of dream thoughts. And in a moment, as though by a bolt of lightning, his mind perked up to the flash of thought that swept across his mind—man's whole life was adumbrated by the bramble bush, the crossing mesh of vicissitudes. You need to be armed to beat them down to make your way through. One thing that kept knocking and buzzing like a fly against the window pane to find entry into the room was the thought of Ruby. He had been putting off something onerous—the letter he intended to write to her. And now, after his exchange of views on what had been an unresolved tangle, the pressure of negligence had mounted. There could be no more dragging of feet. He was too much of a disciplinarian to condone such crass procrastination. He went back to his room, sat down at his writing desk, and began to write on a fresh page of his pad.

Almost two hours passed, and he found the wall clock showing the hands had moved beyond midday when he looked up. Coming up to his door softly, his mother knocked and peeped in. She asked if he would like his coffee sent in since he was so occupied with something important. 'Yes, mama, thank you, but I'm just on the point of winding it up and will join you and Nani on the veranda shortly. But as always, I'd like my coffee to be fresh and hot; and tell Bindia I'd like a ginger nut to go with it.'

Pausing to give the matter good enough thought and to find the right sort of words, it had taken him more time to finish the letter than he thought it should have. The burden of the whole exercise was to bolster Ruby's patience to wait for some more time, the time that, actually, he was buying and whose amount he didn't specify, for he himself didn't quite know. The social and political circumstances were undergoing a whirlwind change. They'd better wait and watch how the coming days unfolded their lives. He was at his wit's end to say anything definite. He would have carried another load had he failed to give her a hint of the looming shadow of what his parents had planned for him. He assured her, though, that he was going to Solan within the next two days to get the house there fully appointed to be in shape to receive her whenever she decided to come and settle in her own house.

In spite of having been driven by the innate truth within him, and with which he had begun the letter, he demurred, perhaps by some queered mental process, and stopped short of revealing to her the details of the whole truth. This, later, as it had with his parents, would gnaw at his mind with a sense of guilt, maybe. He was sure that she had the character to wait with hope and brave adversity if there was going to be any. She would understand even all that he had left unsaid. She had faith in him, and he wasn't ill in using it. He alone, in consonance with his father's wisdom and advice, as his father had by indirection suggested, had to find a solution.

Vikram had initially planned to spend some leisurely time with his friend Madhusudan. However, he changed his plans because he had more pressing matters to attend to. He had some serious concerns that he needed to discuss with his father when he returned from work later in the day. Specifically, Vikram wanted to talk to his father about his plans to go to Solan and complete some finishing touches on his house there.

Before his father returned, Vikram decided to use the few hours he had to cycle up to the main bazaar of Sonepat. His goal was to purchase the items he needed for his journey to Solan and his brief stay at his cottage. He had a lot to do when he got to Solan, and he wanted to ensure he had everything he needed before leaving.

Vikram was aware that his time was limited since he had to return to work soon. Therefore, he decided not to spend another day out with his friends. Instead, he opted to go shopping for the things he needed and focus on finishing his work in Solan. He knew this was the best way to make the most of his limited time off from work.

The headlines in newspapers and the news items covered the arrival of the last Viceroy, Earl Mountbatten, and his flurry of meetings with Indian leaders in the countdown to handing over the power of governance to India's Constituent Assembly; they were drawing up the plans leading to the partition of the country to create Pakistan, the Islamic state and the homeland for the Muslim population, under Muhammad Ali Jinnah, and this had created a general atmosphere of tension among people. Also, it gripped the heart of the general public with apprehension and generated speculation about the future of the country and the expected mass migration of the religiously segregated population.

Side by side, with staunch believers in the two-nation theory and a separate homeland for the Muslims, were large sections of Muslims, who for generations had lived in a Hindu neighbourhood homogeneously, without ever being conscious of any sense of hostility or separate identity on religious grounds. They all lived their life and prayed to their own God in their own way. They could not just think of leaving all their appurtenances of life and going away to some distant place and settling down, deprived of their own land to till. Besides, abandoning the neighbours with whom they had spent their life seemed unthinkable, like with their own kin. It seemed quite outlandish to consider the strange new place their homeland driven by the idea of those considered mentors and responsible for the followers of Islam. Some tales of the idea, and its horrid repercussions happening in trails of blood, travelled far and wide and filled the heart of the peaceful people wherever they belonged with vague fear and insecurity. And such insecurity endemically took root among the people. And so, how could children born within such an infected atmosphere remain unaffected by the atmosphere they breathed in? From this, the idea of identities and the defining lines of the political map of India were generated.

Those politically aware were already preparing to migrate to safety and had already sent the women and children of their families, and movable assets, to areas they deemed safe and convenient. The simple-hearted credibly continued considering the change they saw wrought around by the demon of partition to be short-lived and believed everything would be back to normal after the dust settled on the upheaval-stricken political scene—chiefly in Bengal and Punjab. Vikram was concerned about the situation because his wedded wife was separated from him almost just after the echoes of the wedding bells had fallen silent.

As he was planning and getting ready to go to Solan, his hapless wife still in Gujarat was uppermost in his mind. She was there, left alone to herself and her own devices, to wade through the thick and thin of apprehensions; and he was away from her. His future was yet too foggy for him to be able to write a few words of consolation at a time when she needed them the most. He knew she was faced with such an uncertain tightrope, and he, in his helplessness, could only pray for strength to reach her until he could make arrangements for her to travel up to Solan and fulfil his secret promise to himself.

Yet something he could do, and would do as soon as he boarded the bus to Solan, was to call her up, long distance. Live voice communication would definitely make some difference; however many letters, in their sweep of expressions, may be more inclusive. With such thoughts and cogitations, he got back home with the idea of talking to his father on the first very occasion. His father knew that going to Solan was next on his agenda, but Vikram wanted to finalize his date of departure to Solan and apprise his father of the approximate number of days he may have to spend there for the work to be finished. He was quick to the very first opportunity when he found his father having a stroll, stretching his legs after his day at the office, in the front yard; and he joined him, falling in step. The lengthening shadows of the eucalyptuses across the road streaked across the yard.

'You know, Father, with the number of things that I have on my mind and the numerous agendas to be through with before I leave to go back to join duty, it seems to me that I shall need to extend my leave of absence from work. I shall have to write to the Director General of the Home Office to seek his indulgence. I want to keep the obligation to the minimum and avoid trampling upon the limit. You know, from the kindness they have shown me, how well they hold me in their esteem, especially when they are vexed over the general political turmoil in the country. In fact, I fear anything may happen at any time—the catastrophe of partition. The clouds are ominously dark. Thunder is closing in its rumble, and my fear is that it won't just be rain or squall, but a tornado followed by a cloud burst.'

'You echo my apprehensions, Vicky. Try and make it in a week's time as you have stipulated your stay at Solan. A rivet or nail can be fixed later when you stay there. In the meantime, I shall speed up the preparation for your marriage ceremony, for which the family of Sharmas of Baiyanpur must be eagerly waiting. And I'm sure you know you must do your duty and go through with the formalities without a flicker of sadness on your face at this being an unwilling chore. Most of all, for the sake of Vidya, your would-be bride. She is good-looking with a pleasant expression on her face, ready to smile. Indeed, it would break her heart to see her prospective husband with a grim and surly look. I can understand your sentiment, your reaction, but there are times when you need to play a given role, and you must be a good actor, smother all else but the role the actor has to impersonate.'

'Yes, Father, you are right. But at the same time, perhaps as the great Russian author Tolstoy avers, substantially good simulation, if it goes on over a period of time, can begin to embody the reality of simulation. It is a precarious balancing act—tightrope walking in its true sense. Well, whatever happens, Father, you can rest assured that I shall not let you down, and never forget the moral support I got from you in this grave crisis. And now, considering the paucity of time at our disposal, I think I should, without further delay, leave for Solan tomorrow morning. I'll talk to Mama and you can explain things to her further without, I hope, having to open the bag. Let's go and get some tea. I'm sure you need it more than I do before you go to your easy chair with today's paper, and I go out for a while.'

'All right then, I will get the ladies set about and get the preparations underway so that by the time you return from Solan, the horse with those ornate trappings can be ready for you to ride up to the Baiyanpur reception. Let's go, for the tea must be waiting for us, and your mama must be fretting.'

After tea and the savouries that his mother had made, Vikram felt rejuvenated and called Madhu's to find out if he was available for a ride up to Trio to spend an hour of leisure there. Mrs Bhatia, Madhu's mother, took the call and told Vicky that Madhu wasn't at home; he had to go and meet the Principal of Pali, his sister's college, in connection with her travel schedule with other sportspersons to participate in the university badminton championship. She was an ace at her college. He should have been back by now.

She stopped abruptly and then, after a pause, resumed, 'I'm sorry, but he's just walked in...just hold on...here you are, talk...', and she handed over the receiver to Madhu.

Madhu spoke into the phone, 'Hullo, Vicky, I was wondering what you have been doing with yourself, and I was planning...' and his line of conversation was intruded upon by Vicky.

'I'll tell you, Madhu, and much more. But come and meet me at the Trio if you can make it, and make it snappy.' And he rang off.

He pushed off from the PCO booth outside Bombay Drapery, from where he had been making the call. Not long after he had settled in his favourite seat out on the patio at Trio, he saw Madhu emerging from the tall rear French window. They spotted each other almost at the same moment; they made eye contact and smiled.

'Good. You came along and decided against taking a detour to look up Kailash. I might not have easily got another chance soon to let you know of some important developments at my end. You place the order for coffee and the usual fare while I run over the few important things I shall have to go over in the short leave days that I have. I'm going to Solan tomorrow to get some work done on the house that's coming up there. And I shall be away for no less than a week. On my return, though it doesn't augur well for me, my parents have arranged my marriage with the daughter of a close family friend. I shall, under the obligation of my allegiance and for the occasion particularly, show constrained obedience—and this is strictly between you and me—I shall have to go through with it, what seems to me is no less than an ordeal...the rituals...and not with a poker face, mind you. And the rest, as it is said, is in the hands of God. You and the rest shall be duly informed and, of course, the families honourably invited. Especially you must come to cheer me up. So, while I'm away, just let Balkrishna know. I hope his mother is back home from the hospital—I must find time to visit Aunty. So, he too can take a few days off from the office and come. Kailash won't have to be told twice; such a sweet chap!'

'Yes, we'll see about that. You get the job in Solan done and come back. He's not going anywhere. Like me, he is also a stick in the mud.'

'Oh, come on! Don't undervalue being self-employed. You all enjoy such a lot of independence to do what you like and when you like.'

'The grass must be greener on the other side of the hedge. You can't be wrong, Mr Justice.'

'Now, now! Respect the end of the day. Another round

of coffee, and we shall annoy our moms for being late for dinner. Let's keep the rest for when we are all together. I'm sure there'll be time. Maybe after a week.'

It was quite a while after which they had gotten together, and being together was enough to send a current of good cheer between them. The sound of their laughter turned many a head. They seemed to have been pushing the time of parting, and they quickly left, their smiles slowly wilted into their several concerns like touch-me-not.

Outside, they said 'good night' to each other from their bicycle seats and pedalled off. Madhusudan whistled a tune in undertones; not Vicky. He just looked forward to being on the bus the next morning, where he would have a break long enough to call up Ruby—just as he had promised.

The earliest bus to Solan via Ambala was available at eight in the morning. The bus station was not very far from his residence, and Vikram decided to take the morning bus comfortably after a quick frugal breakfast.

Despite his mind being abuzz with so much and so many things, he still could carry on with banter around the high-swinging preparations for the forthcoming marriage with his mother at the dinner table, holding up his natural pleasant smile. He knew the contrition with which he would be gripped if, by any chance, he said or did anything to hurt her. The nuance of every move of his could not escape his father's notice; he also knew. But on that score, he could bank on his personal understanding with his father. He had travelled thus far only on the strength of his father's tacit and supportive acquiescence, with whom he seemed to have enjoyed a special relationship, a friendliness surpassing the natural filial one.

Running back and forth between the kitchen and the dining table, the maid, Bindia, when she found the chitchat slowly coming to a close, came and stood by Vikram and said with a winsome smile, 'Don't forget this poor girl, Vicky Saab. The gift of my choice would be a true pearl necklace, a matching nose ring and a silk sari.'

And she made everyone laugh in good cheer.

Vikram's 'yes, yes' was lost in the commotion created as everyone got up from their seats to disperse for a while into the sitting room before retiring for the night. The next day's early journey was a good enough reason for Vicky to ask for his leave from his mama to go and hit the bed and leave his parents to themselves.

Vikram set the alarm for six in the morning to ensure he awoke quite in time to check his things. Before he turned in for the night, he made sure that his terse voice emphasised that Bindia rose early to give him his tea and breakfast in good time for him to leave for the bus station. The bus would leave the station at eight, he told her. He went to his father's room after he had said 'good night' to Mama.

In quick time, he thought, he must tell his father what his programme would be like and when, in all probability, he would be back after completing the chores set for the duration of his stay in Solan. Then he left for his own room. He lay down on his bed with thoughts of Ruby. His father could almost see his preoccupation sullying the fair current of awareness of the present, see and understand his intention.

He remembered how, on the side, Vicky couldn't check himself from telling him in a childlike sulk that he'd call Ruby while on a break in his journey; and so, he was glad that his son was intelligent enough to think of all things in their right place, granting that no one could claim to be perfect or totally flawless.

9

In about half an hour, the bus hit the small wayside station of Murthal and passed it by. The Golden Eagle Transport Company thought that stopping at Murthal was just a waste. But the place, Murthal, rang a bell in Vikram's mind from memories of his father's ancient historical account of the neighbourhood areas stretching up to Karnal and beyond. It was ancient land associated with the great epic war, the *Mahabharata*. There was a lake, a water body associated with the character of Karna, who, having been born on the wrong side of the blanket and abandoned by his mother, Kunti, spent most of his life in search of a valid identity until he was anointed as the ruler of Anga by Duryodhana, the heir apparent of the glorious kingdom of Hastinapur. And he expressly took this bold step without the imperial permission of the sightless caretaker king of the kingdom of Hastinapur, his father, as the purchase of the pledge of the lifelong friendship of a superb bowman and a fearless warrior.

Within himself, though, Karna always felt like an abandoned child and a foundling. All life, he owed a filial allegiance to the lower caste, a coachman, and also a fish monger, a man and wife who had reared him and had given him all that parents naturally give their child; and he wore the badge of a stigma of being a lowborn, though the attributes of his superior class shone through the several humiliating situations he had to face in life. Not the least of them all was being the first choice of Draupadi at her swayamvar. But for a sly signal of being forbidden from her well-wisher and friend, Krishna, she would have given a sharp twist to the following events of history by marrying Karna.

Murthal, he recalled his father telling him, was the distortion of the ancient name from the *Mahabharata*. It was located on the edge of the great cauldron of carnage, the Kurukshetra battlefield, where in a battle of eighteen days, close to two million troops perished; it is also the place of the disposal of the dead who fell fighting on the battlefield, and was literally called Marusthal. He had gone on to say that they were living almost inside the borders of the vast and prosperous kingdom of Hastinapur. On his journey towards Solan, he would be travelling through the land where epoch-defining events played out and were celebrated by Veda Vyasa in his epic, the *Mahabharata*.

And so, along the Grand Trunk Road, the bus raced ahead, flanked by the greenery of loaded wheat crops, paddy fields and taller corn fields. On the roadside and away from the busy road connecting the big cities, the bus passed by some big and small, inhabited, flourishing villages.

Going past growing townships like Samalkha, he noticed bullock carts more frequently, even horse carts swaying, loaded with farm products, kicking up a lot of dust on the country roads. He also noticed that as his bus touched the next big town of Panipat, tall chimneys came up, spouting dark puffs of smoke; the air of dusty towns was becoming polluted with factory smoke from the growing industry. As he approached towns like Panipat, Karnal and Ambala, there were several more such factories, cemented tall buildings with sloping roofs and corrugated galvanised iron sheets and chimneys. He was not surprised to notice that the name of this town was spelled as 'Umbala', which he saw embossed and preserved on an old gateway pillar of the railway station. In passing Karnal, he was told by a better-informed gentleman passenger that this was a full-fledged and flourishing industrial area, where processing of milk and milk products was carried out and where the cheese he relished so much in his breakfast came from.

As he had planned to make a long-distance call to Ruby back in Gujarat, he decided to take his coffee break at Ambala, in the station's restaurant. He stepped out of the bus along with some other passengers and felt as though an unpleasant smell of horse stables had hit him. Indeed, there were a couple of tongas, popular for local conveyance, and the diesel fumes, too, were emanating from the ceaseless movement of a host of buses coming into and going out of the busy bus station of Ambala. But he, with his nose buried in his handkerchief, hurried his way to the restaurant entrance after having climbed a flight of stairs up to the first floor to the glazed dining area.

It was just a half-hour stop. But after his coffee and a bite of biscuit, he felt relaxed. The warm summer days were here, and outside, the sky blazed in spite of the haze of dust and smoke. He came down to board the bus and found that he was one of the first few passengers to get into the comfort of his seat after the break. Within minutes, the driver was back at the steering and seemed to be enjoying the drive through the verdurous land of Punjab, with villages looking prosperous and growing with modern electronic gadgetry, flicking and blaring country and popular film music from roadside shops as the bus passed by. The towns of Dera Bassi and later Zirakpur showed definite signs of town culture. There were hospitals with signs of the Red Cross and school buildings alive with boys and girls in their uniforms. On the roads, some young people could be sighted in bright-coloured or bold-striped t-shirts and blue denim drainpipes, and some of them on their new acquisition, a motorcycle, flaunting their locks like film actors.

Even a casual glance out of the window of a moving bus, especially for someone who happened to pass through this familiar landscape after a long while, couldn't but be struck by the occasional few patches of orange standing bright in the midst of green flowing fields. A few bigger farmers, it seemed, showed enterprise and invested exclusively in rearing orchards of big juicy citrus fruit, a cross between tangerine and orange, locally called 'malta'. It made Vikram truly happy and not a little proud to see how the farmers, in remote areas too, experimented with fresh ideas and made inroads into the vegetable markets of nearby cities with a variety of fruit, full of delectable and healthy juice. At Zirakpur and beyond, city life began to be veritably evident in every way, in apparel and conduct of people in public and the drivers on the road. Even the truck drivers strictly followed the road safety rules. On highways, whether day or night, truck drivers have always been better-behaved drivers. Their caution may, at times, seem overdone. They take good care to give respectable distance to the cops, and to avoid any messes, maybe because of dubious freight.

From Mohali onwards, the skyline began to look like the typical silhouetted and broken skyline of the city. Passing through an aura of mixed smells of the city, the bus wound its way through the outskirts of the local village until it hit the main road. Shopping arcades busy with Punjab's fashion-conscious crowds from the higher end of society could be glimpsed walking in and out of the revolving entrances and through the glazed windows of the shops. Vicky's heart began to beat slightly faster as the bus braked in its bay. The doors opened and in swarmed the usual bus stop smells—food barely covered, the fumes of diesel emission, swarms of buzzing flies, and people began to move out. Vikram, too, sidled into the single-person queue. He had spotted a row of five telephone booths as soon as he set his foot down on the platform and made a beeline to the last one in the row, which he thought would provide him with an early chance into it, and maybe a quieter corner than the others. Not far wrong in his guesses, he was able to get his chance in five minutes. He booked a long distance, and within a couple of minutes, he heard Ruby's voice, eager and choked with emotion, calling out loudly 'hullo'.

Her 'hullo' ended in a suppressed sob until she heard Vikram saying, 'Hullo, sweetheart' to her, in his affection-soaked voice, consoling her, and added, 'Oh, it seems such a long while since I've talked to you. Hope all's well.' And to calm her down, he tried to be casual and reassuring. 'Oh, come on, Rubyianka (he fondly called her by this foreign-sounding twist to her name; and she smiled, as usual, he imagined, and he smiled too). We don't want to spend the little time we have in the shared and well-understood sentiment. I know how difficult and painful, and from personal experience, every moment of your lonely separation must be. But the redeeming fact is that I'm going to Solan to get the job on our home finally done so that I can tell you to come over as early as possible.'

He heard some more snivelling sobs and could imagine her wiping her nose and eyes with her minuscule handkerchief. She could not talk much, and whatever the situation might be, he knew that she would never blame him for the distance and his delay in getting them back together. And not speaking made it doubly painful, the confinement. Besides being duty hours, he knew she must be taking the call from the Matron's cubicle, and she knew the limits of her liberty. In quick parting words, he told her to take courage from the fact that even in separation, they were still in touch with each other and understood the compulsions of the predicament, which indeed was rather complicated. To stay put in such adverse circumstances and the growing tension in the social and political atmosphere was finally going to be their triumph in a union.

'So, we'll both have to brave intervening pauses with the courage of our love and grin and bear it!'

He was glad to notice she had gained some equipoise, for she said, 'Mummy and Pop send you their love and remember you a lot in several situations at the table and in the lounge.'

'Thanks, indeed. And do please convey my respectful regards and great love to dear Alva and loving and kind Mr Constantine. I've given my father a general picture of the developments there and received his ready approval of the things as they are. His good wishes and blessings for the days to come are with us. I wish—at the present moment, and I've never had such a wild wish before—I had some supernal power to make things happen soon as you desire them such as Aladdin could hold occult powers with his lamp.' And he laughed shortly at himself.

Ruby didn't join him. This, she thought, was no time for such frivolity. Her future in her confounded mind loomed like a huge question mark. Even after talking to her husband and hearing his practical plans, she continued to feel uneasy. The rub here was that there was no definite timeframe for the plans to come through to their desired conclusion.

Deciding finally that there was no other way out, either that she could think of or suggested by Vikram. With the idea not to be any cause of even the mildest hint of deflation of the spirit of assurance with which Vikram was going to Solan, she raised her voice a couple of notches in cheer when she spoke.

'Well, let us pray that your mission at Solan is accomplished sooner than you scheduled. Until then, we must muster our grit and patience to wait for happy days. Wish you all the best that you go through the job smoothly without getting harrowed anyway. So mind your temper, darling; this is a "bon voyage"! Do call up a bit more frequently. Hope to see you soon, darling.'

She put the telephone receiver down in its cradle. And sat there in the Matron's cubicle, throttling the sobs threatening to rise to her throat, lest she create a scene. It took her a while before she could gather her wits and emerge from the cubicle to face her colleagues and the other members of the staff.

While Vikram, on his side, smiled slightly with a new glow in his impressive blue eyes, glad that Ruby, his Ruby, had truly turned out to be a real ruby, sanguine and of true inherent strength. Unwillingly, with five or six people in sight from the corner of his eye outside in a queue, he pushed open the glass door of the booth and emerged with half a smile, fighting off his embarrassment at having kept them all waiting. He was possessed by the very short time that he could talk to Ruby. Bolstering his morale at the conclusion, he felt it did make up for the touch-and-go conversation. And indeed, there seemed to be buoyancy in his step as he turned back to the bus in its bay. He made the briefest stopover on his way at a soft drink counter to buy himself a lemony 7up to wet his dried whistle.

For a long while, as the bus wound its way through turnings of the city roads and the last lap of level land, he had a close and clear look at the foothills of Simla, wrapped in a distant mist of dark green, covered with evergreens and pine woods. He remained entangled in the warp and woof of what he'd said to Ruby and what had been left unsaid, going over and over the mixed emotions, the joy and regret of the moment. So engrossed he remained that he hardly knew when he went by the turning on the side of Panchkula towards Kalka.

He missed out on watching his bus run past the upcoming sprawling manufactories of Hindustan Machine Tools as well as the adjoining compound that was to house the company's employees. For a patch of about a mile or more, the railway line ran parallel to the road, not very far from each other, so that both the rail and bus travellers could, from their vantage, notice the tall chimney spewing out thick clouds of smoke from the Cement Factory close to Rajpur station. He had not yet been able to gather his thoughts and come out of his reverie when Vikram passed by the well-known Pinjore Mughal Garden and the town itself as the bus began the climb from the precincts of Kalka into the heart of the town.

After the jolting bumps over frequent speed breakers, the bus left the last post in the foothills behind and took a sharp turn onto the road to Solan. The change in the landscape and the topography alongside the road would take him and his fellow travellers to Solan in about two-and-a-half to three hours. Vikram seemed to have emerged from his obfuscated thoughts to see shifting images outside the window. The continuum of mental conversation with another image that of Ruby in his mind, like strains of background music, had ceased and been replaced with the subdued roar and screech of tyres around sharp turnings. He saw and could make out the small wayside temple with a red conical flag on its small, rectangular but conically tapering spire just beyond the newly come-up industrial area of Parwanu in the flatland alongside the nondescript waterway, which turned over the rounded-stone-rich mountain rill to meet the larger Jhajjar.

Soon he found himself deeply engaged in going over the list of building materials he would have to order. In his reckoning, he thought he would have just enough time for a cup of tea after he set foot down at Solan's bus stop before he had to walk down to the market to place his order for all the building accessories. He would only be able to make out the list in black and white when he reached his destination. On the spot, in the midst of the unfinished work on the homestead he was planning, he would be in a better position to muster the details of things when he'd have his architect by his side to complement and finalize the list of purchases to make. He could then be confident of not leaving any loopholes. He, therefore, decided that instead of taking any step by himself, he would get in touch with his architect first thing after he reached Solan.

The whole fabric of planning that had gone on as his bus closed in on Solan went out of the window by the time his bus came to a stop.

He got down in quite a different frame of mind and walked straight towards the main road entrance to the Sood ABC Store to say 'hullo' to Rahul and hand over the list of provisions he would require for his morning tea and breakfast the next morning, besides, of course, the groceries for about the next ten days that he would need to spend in Solan. The first thing that he needed was a refreshing drink, and he bought orangeade without fizz for himself and sipped it slowly as he walked into the interior of the shop.

After a cordial meeting, he briefly told Rahul about his general plans and sat down in the corner chair shown to him. He gladly accepted his welcome offer to have tea with him there. Having shaken off a bit of the stiffness of the long bus journey in the hot June sun, he got up from the comfort of his chair. Rahul had arranged for a boy to carry Mr Rana's two bags to his cottage. Nimble on his feet, the young fellow scrambled and reached the cottage about fifteen minutes before Vikram, who took it easy and enjoyed the sights of the sunbathed hilltops in the setting sun and the valleys filed with thin grey mist.

He breathed in the fresh mountain air and walked up to the half-finished cottage that stood out like a sore thumb. There, he promised himself that he would complete the cottage in the time that he would be there. *Soon, he would arrive with his bag and baggage and maybe a bride to settle down in the neighbourhood*, Vikram thought.

Motiram, the caretaker Vikram had left in the servant quarters on the estate, came to greet him, and Vikram exchanged pleasantries with him. Vikram told him what he would like for his dinner. Motiram could still go to the market and get whatever would be required by his wife Parvati to get Vikram's meal ready in good time. He was glad to see that Motiram had cleaned up the room he had kept locked for his personal use. After a quick wash, he sat down to business. He telephoned Hiralal Sood to find out if his architect nephew, Durgadas, was available. He was back in Solan to conclude the whole lot of work left to be done on his cottage and would need him almost constantly to carry out whatever had to be done without any waste of time. Vikram was glad to know that Durgadas, who had been out all day on another site, was just back. He arrived and Vikram was crisp and precise in giving his instructions. He told Durgadas to dig up all the relevant papers, especially the blueprints of the drawings of the cottage when he would come the next morning. The false ceiling all along the roof had yet to be fixed, he reminded him.

'Since I'm hard pressed for time—I'm on a leave of absence and due to report back on duty—I would request you to somehow make adjustments to your schedule; of course, taking your customers into your confidence so that you are able to devote a maximum of your time to the work here and finish the job,' he said to Durgadas. And he added, 'Take a quick look at the total work yet to be done. Money is not much of a bother, so get all the materials you need as you go over from item to item on the agenda. Employ all the men you require, but we have to fix the last glass on the inside panels of the wardrobes and finish the last touch of the paint and varnish on the doors and windows before the end of the month when I leave.' He spoke warmly. 'May God bless us with success. I will see you tomorrow morning. Godspeed! Polish off the sweets on your plate and take the rest of the packet back home for the family. There is a kilo of mangoes for you. Motiram will give you the bag. Take it home,' he concluded and got up, indicating the end of the business meeting.

Vikram indicated to Motiram to get his bath ready. He

preferred to wash and be refreshed before having a small drink, prior to sitting down to eat his last meal. It would be a good idea to hit the bed early because, from the next day onwards, he was going to be fully occupied at all hours of the day. Since the work would be in progress in the house, he may be forced to skip his siesta. He shall have to do with minimum relaxation, and so, would not perhaps get to the few pages of the detective novel that he had brought with him and was accustomed to reading before he fell asleep. He was glad though that he had been able to get hold of the key man, his architect, and had apprised him of what limitations they were working under. He was aware of so many other obligations to which he was committed to at Sonepat and back in Gujarat. Thinking of which, for once, at least his heart sank.

'Ruby, O Ruby!' he murmured softly to himself, with a hint of melancholy in his voice.

He felt sad and helpless, though he could still take courage from the fact that his father was ever there to support him. Yet he could not help feeling depressed and limp in the context of the very private predicament that he had so self-assuredly created for himself and now seemed to be in. There was a fast-rising level of morass around him. It took herculean effort to get out of the state of mind that he found himself sinking into.

And out of the blue, in his mind flashed the cheerful lit-up dining hall of the ancient mansion in which was the restaurant where he had stopped for lunch. He had heard of the renown of the food that was served there since the time of the British. And indeed, there were black and white pictures of beautiful young English ladies and uniformed mustachioed men decorating the walls, among other images of beautiful landscapes covering misted valleys and sunlit mountain tops. In keeping with tradition, there was subdued (recorded) piano music playing and waiters were serving at tables in their frayed liveries. But the noise created by the children and chattering women and their men tamely going and coming from washrooms were the same as usual in any other wayside restaurant. The remembrance of the cheerful ambience pushed him further into the dumps.

He hurried through his shower and the warm bath that rid him of the clammy feeling and rubbed himself down with his clean towel. It made him feel slightly better by the time he dressed up and sat for his dinner. Simple fare though it was, but having been freshly cooked and served steaming hot by Motiram, it not only smelled good but also whetted his appetite. He ate to his fill. And instead of any regular dessert, he told Motiram to fetch him a cup of hot milk, sweet and strongly flavoured with cocoa, which he sometimes took as his nightcap.

10

The next morning, by the time Vikram finished his coffee after breakfast he could hear activity had begun outside. From his window, he could see the labourers climbing the trail in their practised slow steps, carrying large sleepers of timber and board. There was a lot of work to be done on the floors and the false ceiling, all along the roof made of corrugated and galvanised sheets in both the main building and the annexe. Some sturdy men carried cans of adhesive and several tin cans of paint, smaller boxes of all sizes of nails, screws and nuts and other oils needed for the walls of the ceiling. The materials were all available at Hiralal's store. For the lumber, too, they didn't have to go far to look for it. It was procured from the neighbouring Goyal Timber Merchant's stock. Goyal had an electric saw with which he shaped the boles and shafts according to the required sizes and designs of the customers.

As it was the first day of construction work, the carpenters and other skilled labour all accompanied Durgadas. As though already trained and instructed, they fell to their saws and hammers and other measuring tools, and the work began in earnest, which by its tempo seemed it had never stopped.

As the proceedings got underway, Vikram felt a pleasant jab of joy stirring him. He felt that, by God's kindness, the whole thing—his mission of the arduous journey and the rest, appeared to augur well in its good beginning. And within himself, Vikram appreciated Durgadas for setting the wheels into motion. For it also assured Vikram that Durgadas really understood the spirit of the instruction he had given him last evening, and the work would indeed be accomplished in good time.

A little early next morning, Vikram, after he'd had his morning cup of tea, decided to get in touch with the District Magistrate Nardev Shastri, with whom he had sat on a division bench during his last visit. They had been part of the hearing of that important case of the Punjab States versus the richest transporters of potatoes and apples from Narkanda and Kotgarh and liquor, especially the brand produced by Meakin Breweries in a suburb of Solan. The Taj Transport Company owned the largest fleet of vehicles, plying their trucks and buses between Narkanda and Delhi. Of late, with the establishment of a government degree college in the capital of the small state, Rampur Bushahr, on the border of Kangra district and the banks of the young boulder-bedded Sutlej River, ruled by local ruler Narsingh Bahadur, the company had extended its bus route to have a junction terminal stoppage at Rampur. It joined the district of Kinnaur further ahead up to Sarahan.

Vikram liked the magistrate as he was a good human being. And mentally, he had a vague sort of plan to meet him and revive his brief acquaintance and see if it could evolve into a warm friendship between them. Indeed, his coming to stay in Solan in the neighbourhood of the gentleman was not the only reason for the overture he was planning. He was looking forward to creating an opportunity for the beginning of a career, in case he took early retirement as he had once thought he would, and privately his plan still was to do. And who could be of better help than one who was a fellow walker in the profession of law? A local, and one whose words of ripened wisdom were eminently held in the esteem of the people. Besides, he was a good human being; amiable and, Vikram hoped, sympathetic.

He was quite candid in his intentions and had decided to frankly tell Nardev what exactly was in his mind. He wished to follow his search and explore the smaller kingdoms in the hinterland, but not too far from Solan. He decided to tell Nardev all as truly and honestly and say that he looked up to him for his suggestion, advice and assistance in his search for getting anchored in a place of his liking.

So, after he had finished his coffee, post a belated breakfast, he ascertained the time from the wristwatch he wore; whether or not the time was right for a telephone call to Nardev. For intrusion upon Nardev's engagement in the middle of a case at court was the last thing he would allow himself to venture. He knew how badly such a misadventure, like a freak telephone call in the middle of an important hearing, would cause an unpardonable seismic jolt to the sensitive mind of a magistrate.

Vikram knew that at the hour of 1.00 p.m., the court would adjourn for its lunch break and Nardev would be, for at least the next hour, in his chamber. He decided to put through his call to him right on the dot. It would be a surprise for him to know that Vikramjit Rana was in town in person. He had called him up the week before last when the date of his departure hadn't been finalized. He, therefore, had told him about his plans to journey up to Solan but hadn't given any particular date of his arrival.

He was still smacking his lips after his last draught of orange juice when he dialled Nardev's personal number. Within a minute, he heard the receiver at the other end being lifted and Nardev, in his very cultured and soft voice, spoke across the wires. 'Hullo, it's Nardev Shastri here. May I know who's calling please?'

Vikram was thrilled to get Nardev right away. 'Hullo, Nardev, Vikram Rana at this end. I arrived last evening and thought of you. But I knew you would be at work, yet I was wondering when you'd have a little free time for me to come over and talk to you.'

'I'm going to be preoccupied until half past four in the afternoon; after which I have a little time to be home, especially with my old man, senior Mr Shastri. He's crossed ninety but waits for me to spend a few minutes with him and share some interesting story from the courts with a smile. I never miss a rejoinder from him. It brightens up his day.

But come, Neeti will be happy to meet you. Come over any time after seven in the evening and stay for a bite after we've talked over our drink together. I hope it suits you?'

'Anything you say.' Vikram laughed in good cheer, and Nardev joined in. 'I'll keep time. After seven then. In the meanwhile, greet your old man with my regards until I meet him personally.'

'Looking forward to seeing you, brother,' he said, and hung up. Nardev was not much given to demonstrate an overt sense of humour, but he was a good judge of character. So, even if there could not be a backslapping friendship, there did exist a mutually warm relationship and a feeling of camaraderie.

Vikram slipped into a light jacket and prepared to go down to the bus plaza to just stretch his legs and familiarize himself with the neighbourhood. Slightly up towards the market, as he emerged from the wicket gate leading up to his cottage, he saw the shoeshine boy sitting in front of the chemist's—owned by a retired old army man, Manmohan Singh Siddhu. The shop went by the popular name of 'Siddhu Chemist'. Vikram greeted the Sardar with 'Sat Sri Akaal' in Punjabi style, and put his left foot up on the shoe slope on the box of his appurtenances behind which the boy had sat. The boy took the hint and, as a first step to give the shine, he dusted the shoes with a large brush and then began to go step by step, applying polish and cream and colour wherever it was indicated to be used. Steadily, having finished one shoe, he gave a double knock on the slope with the wooden part of the brush to indicate that finishing touches were now required on the second shoe. Vikram felt satisfied with the work of the youngster and gave him a handsome tip. He smiled and proceeded further on, but he saw the boy smile and say, 'Thank you' before he took his first long stride in the direction of the market.

On the opposite side of his favourite haunt, the Sood ABC, he saw a small shop with a signboard above the narrow entrance at the end of a three-step climb. The legend was a bit weird. 'Soda Fizz' it said. Its narrow interior had but two small tables with two seats each. And upon the stunted counter sat the soda machine, and the vendor stood behind it. He made fresh lemon juice and gave it a shot of fresh soda before it was served. All this in the end was not much different from the lemonade commonly served on any cold drinks' counter, save for the connoisseur of ultra-sharp sense organs that could detect the pungency and the tangy barb in the nostril. It had no added flavours, but the sniffling sting of fresh lemon juice and the oils from the peel as you sipped it. That perhaps was the secret of its being extra refreshing, a welcome drink on one of the warm days, even at the height of five thousand feet above sea level, where Solan is located.

Vikram enjoyed his lemonade with that extra punch to it, smiled at the owner of the stall and climbed down the steep stairs to the road level. A glance up at the road, men and women out in bright reds, yellow and greens and men in their morning trousers livened up the scene in the warm sun and cool mountain breeze. There was a rich and balmy aroma from the pine forests along the mountain slopes, which were interspersed with tall cedars, reaching up to the very clear and blue sky. One could see women from the interior villages carrying a whole gamut of fruits and vegetables, all their farm produce, in kiltàs, conical baskets slung on their backs, in the morning. They were now going back with their kiltas still slung on their back, not entirely empty. There were provisions of daily use available and bought at a grocers' in the town. Little beads of sweat shone on their fair complexioned faces gone darker pink with exertion and midday sun, but their colourful headdresses were tidily placed over their combed black hair as they trudged back home. It was, after all, an enjoyable day out, especially after the sale and purchase and the spicy samosas and some sweets like jalebi in the streets of Solan.

He strolled up to the plaza of the bus station and just allowed his eyes to go idly around a routine busy scene, enjoying the sight of locals mingling with the passengers going in and coming out of the stuffy restaurant of Sardarji. He lounged around and then entered Sood ABC to get the latest on the political scene in Delhi, the hotbed of political activity, on the radio. He would have a casual word or two with Rahul before returning to his cottage for his afternoon rest. Whatever else may engage his attention and wherever he might be, he must, by custom, get back home to sit at his midday meal at around 1.30 p.m.

He was glad to notice that Durgadas was diligently supervising the work that was in progress inside of the annexe as he passed by, and found the workers earnestly at the job around the house as he reached the last few cemented steps to the entrance. Satisfied with the work, he relaxed and got ready to eat.

Noticing Mr Rana walking up to the cottage, Durgadas too followed, walking behind him. And it was almost like a reflex on the part of Vikram, and he turned around and said, 'What about your lunch? I wonder if you'd care for a bite here with me? I'm sure the workers are given a lunch hour break so that they can eat and rest a while.'

'It is from half-past-one to half-past-two that the workers get their time off. They keep to their timing,' he said. 'My wife waits for me to get back home to have our lunch together. The routine has become something of a habit. I shall invite you to come over for a meal together. Urmi, my wife, will be glad to make something special for you, maybe halwa and puris and matar pulao, all homely delicacies, with home-made pickles.'

And they laughed as they entered the sitting room.

'Oh, I'd love it. Yes, we shall surely make it before I leave Solan also after the work here is completed. In your hands, I'm sure you'd see that it is done.'

It was a suggestive remark, but they both enjoyed the joke behind it. After whatever little business talk Durgadas had wanted to have with the master, he politely left.

It was a pleasure to sluice his face. Vikram felt refreshed. And not long afterwards, Motiram came to find out if the master was ready to eat and had the lunch served. Vikram sat at the head of an oblong dinner table with six chairs in an airy room. Within the next half hour, he was fast asleep in his bed, made by the deft housekeeper and cook Parvati.

Sunbeams were steeply slanted by the time Vikram turned in his bed. But he blinked his eyes a few times before he opened them to a brightly lit room. The light of the sun was declining into the western horizon.

The entrance of the cottage faced slightly west of the north; the mountain ranges were away, beyond wide and shallow valleys, and so, the rooms were floodlit both in the mornings and the evenings, at the time of sunrise and sunset. The thought of going to see Nardev on the eastern slope, of a spur of the main Solan hill, made him alert. He was halfway through having his afternoon tea.

On his way, as he walked down through a part of the market at about half past six, he got a case of five kilograms of mangoes packed and got a straggling daily wager to carry the case of mangoes up to the DM's house. The man readily agreed and, without waiting for instructions, he proceeded towards the residence of the Magistrate in quick and short steps. Vikram followed the man a little distance behind. Urmila Shastri opened the door to the porter who carried the case of mangoes to the doorstep; he had got there just a couple of minutes before Vikram reached. She greeted Vikram at the door, 'Welcome, Mr Rana. Come in please, my husband is waiting for you.'

'Good to see you Ma'am, and how's the family?'

'We're all doing fine. But as you know, living in the dread of the shadow of partition. By and large, life here goes on as usual. The shops in the bazaars are busy with the usual everyday sights.'

Having disposed of the coolie, Vikram followed Mrs

Shastri into the corridor that led to the sitting room. Urmila led the way into the room saying, 'Here's your Barrister friend, and he has brought some luscious mangoes for you.'

Nardev got up from his seat on his comfortable sofa next to the window. He came forward and hugged Vikram and offered and urged him to be seated in that comfortable sofa seat that he had occupied. It was his preferred vantage, with a view from a couple of windows on his side of the wall. The first glance outside showed him a bed of white and pink roses, overhung by the large bushy plant of cosmos, full of starry little white flowers. It gladdened Vikram's heart. He turned round to respond to Nardev's enquiry, 'How was your journey? How long is your stay going to be?'

'It was wonderful. I have not yet decided how long I will stay. Let me see,' Vikram replied nonchalantly.

'Oh, good. The sun felt more than just warm until we entered the hill country after Pinjore Gardens and the industrial Parwanu. We then got a whiff of the cool mountain air. Some familiarity with the places on the way made the experience more enjoyable; more so with the break and short stoppage at Barog for lunch. The passengers got out to stretch their legs and get a breath of the fresh and smoke-free mountain air with its faint aroma of pines and cedars on the slopes.'

'Good that you had time enough to enjoy the sights and smells better. The change of landscape and topography at each turn makes it interesting. And then the silence of the mountains is overwhelming.'

'Oh yes. It is such a relief to the senses to leave the memories of the sordid and crooked-striated cities. Oh, there's such a rat race going on down there, in which perhaps only Lucifer would revel.'

And they both laughed at Vikram's witty remark.

'But, dear barrister, the courtrooms are still full of the muck from what you call the sordid city streets. All that doesn't let us forget the world of which we are a part. They keep the devil's workshop going down there, and we continue to get our bread and butter.'

Once again, they laughed at the subtle humour in what Nardev had said.

'The fresh mangoes available close to Panckula were juicy and plump, more attractive, but it would have been unfair on my part to have stopped the bus to make a purchase. But thanks to the advances in the transport system, those I bought here don't seem much different in appearance and I do hope they taste as good.'

'Well, well it was really sweet of you to have thought of us. Thank you very much. I'm sure my father would love to have a taste of them right away. He's so fond of mangoes since his childhood. He happened to spend the early years of his boyhood close to the mango orchards in Lucknow, where his father was teaching medicine at the local medical college. But, here, just sample some of these peaches and fresh figs from our orchard in Rajgarh, about forty miles from here.'

A maid had brought a plate full of some fruits and placed it on the table in front of them.

'How much has the politically agitated atmosphere in

our capital affected, or shall I say, contaminated, the clear air of the hills? The sheer lure of the political power of the ambitious political novices, in their public utterances, gives me the impression that, to a considerable extent, they have been successful in having created a definite idea of the insurmountable chasm of division in the society on religious grounds. But the most unfortunate part is the ensuing hardened bifurcation. Even some eminent leaders of the communities have been obsessed with the idea. They drill it into the gullible mind of the polity that it is all due to the incompatibility of the two faiths. And go on to put their seal on the parochial dictum of the improbability of the communities to ever live together. Because they aver and preach, the two religious groups are indeed separate nations and so must have separate homelands—as delineated and demanded by Choudhry Rahmat Ali...

'Sorry for this dilatory digression, but do bear with me a while. What I was going to say was that such warped logic, quite contrary to the living proof of history, may be pardonably acceptable among the uninitiated and the ignorant, but pity is the fountainhead of the elite and learned Islamic scholars, the moulvis. The pandits too have not cared to give commonalty the correct exposition and tolerant aspects of scriptures. The attitude seems to be equally bad on both sides. Bigotry has led to the extremity of bloodshed and ugly violence among neighbours.

'Even recent history is witness to the harmonious existence of the communities in towns and villages, to the extent that there's evidence of mutual sharing of cultural and religious events and marriage ceremonies and even an exchange of gifts on such occasions.'

Nardev said, 'I can understand the fervour underlying your idealism. Gandhi's version is tempered with much more tolerance and forgiveness, and he has to be followed if we look forward to the invocation of peace. Questioning and reasoning, more quibbling, will go on endlessly, and so will the ensuing acrimony and violence. Come now, I have some good single malt, or would you like something more fashionable like vodka; but what I have is a Japanese variety.'

'I'll be conservative in choice. I'll go for whiskey any day and my choice stops at single malt. I'd prefer it with a dash of soda and ice.'

'A very British choice! I like to have mine on the rocks. You can munch on a peach or an apricot while I fetch the drinks.'

There was the clink of glass and ice from the adjacent room while Vikram admired the fresh flavours of the peaches and figs. To the fork, the apricots seemed a bit hard and unripe. And while he was sampling the farm-fresh fruits, Nardev returned with a silver-plated salver with two drinks. 'To a lively future together at Solan,' said Nardev and they sipped their drinks, and Vikram indicated his appreciation of the quality of the whiskey by raising his left eyebrow.

'It's always great to have the single malt but to have it along with you is a privilege.' Vikram's remark followed.

The maid brought a plate of chicken dumplings and left the gentlemen. Urmila didn't seem to be coming out to join them, perhaps busy in the kitchen with dinner preparations. Vikram found an opportunity to open up with his intent, the drag of hesitancy nevertheless followed as he sought a favour. Yet, being a forthright man, he knew and had decided before he came over to Nardev that the best way would be to be candid about the whole matter. He, therefore, opened the conversation. 'You can largely understand, Nardev, the causes that led me up to decide to settle down here in Solan. Let me spell it out by saying that the deciding factor is the impending partition of the country, which now is almost certain. And indeed, it shall be a calamitous occurrence. Considering the climate and landscape, it suits my temperament, and the endowment of the piece of land was truly a blessing and I finally decided to go plump for Solan. Of prime importance would be a vocation concomitant with the education that I've had, with a rider of my very personal preferences.

'By our education and training we have both been groomed for a vocation in law. It was your natural wisdom, and added to it was your father's guidance of experience, which you diligently abided and pursued and sat for the competitive exam for State Judiciary Service and made it to the selection list. The judiciary of the state and the country would be proud of an officer like you. My prodding the higher echelons has not been favourably responded to with any hopeful indication. For a bar at law from Middle Temple, Lincoln's Inn, England, there is nothing suitable yet, and for some time to come. My parents have fixed my marriage exactly after ten days from now, that is, for the 23rd of this month.'

'Well,' Nardev toasted, 'that's great news and I'm going to stop you for a moment from going on and raise a toast to the forthcoming many-times-over happy conjugal union.'

They raised their glasses and took a deep draught of the drinks and hugged each other in good cheer. Nardev's laughter expressed his joy for Vikram's future life, but Vikram's smile, even though broad, concealed an admixture of inscrutable emotions, which Nardev didn't notice—nor had he any inclination but to take it as sheer joy.

'I have decided to put in my papers as soon as convenient and come and settle down here,' Vikram said. 'But here's the rub. My conclusion, at the end of all cogitations, is that there couldn't be anyone better than you to discuss the matter with. All told, one thing is certain—no more British masters. I would not like to serve the English Crown anymore, and you can attribute this to the influence of Gandhi, particularly his voice of protest against British rule of the rod against the non-violent marches of the justifiably aggrieved poor workers on the farms and in the mills and factories. My mind is filled with revulsion for the arrogant rulers when I think of how the merciless reign of police terror is let loose on them at the drop of a hat, perhaps more from their own frustration in dealing with the firm and strictly lawful non-violent resistance.'

'Oh, forget it, brother,' Nardev added. 'Don't let unnecessary bitterness contaminate your mind. The imperialist and expansionist attitude of the British, which they camouflage in Christian charity, is now an open secret. Claiming to bring light and grace of faith and education, their ambition burgled the ancient civilisations of the Orient of much more than material wealth. They destroyed and denuded the sanctum sanctorum of almost all age-old venerated temples of their riches, and left the repositories and epicentres of our ancient culture in mere shells. All resentment is but shadow-boxing with the remains of vicarious catharsis. Curse though the partition is for the subcontinent, it is inevitable as the point of no return has been reached regarding political negotiations. And in the face of the headstrong stand of both Jawaharlal and Jinnah, even Gandhi seems to have given up in despair. So just as I said, for now, forget it all as the inexorable and give your mind to what I have in my mind. I have a suggestion that might provide a meaningful direction for your present predicament. But I need to first put it across to you as a mere idea. You can take it up for more serious consideration after having given it some thought. Come, let me give you a broad outline of the idea.'

'I'm sorry for the interruption,' Vikram began. 'You know, Nardev, I had some vague inkling, a modern psychological scientist would perhaps call it wishful thinking, but even Confucius avers that to clear the way to find the truth of things, the prime thing is to call things by their right name and keep your mind clear of confusion. Yes, let me continue with what I was intending to tell you. I was stuck with a serious problem. To resolve it would also mean to make a decision of a lifetime. I found that I needed help. And the help I needed was from someone who would not need a lot of explaining to, someone with not only cumulative wisdom from the variegated experience of living but also sympathetically inclined. As the naturally logical next step, I was led to think of you, with almost certainty of hope that

I shall not have to look any further. So, let's have it. I can hardly wait for you to lay out your idea.'

Nardev began. 'What I'm going to present to you is what I've gathered from what you have been saying all along, and as I understood from what you have said and how you have said. Considering all that, there was something already in my mind that sparked off and evolved into something meaningful. Let me put it into the simplest words. One, you have, for definitely good reasons, decided to settle down here in Solan. Two, coming after your marriage, you'd start your family here. Three, you have decided to resign from your very respectable and well-paid job, and not to take up work under the government. Yet, getting a vocational occupation that is substantially lucrative, commensurate with your credentials, is imperative to maintain your standard of living and social standing. Four, and this, I presumed and I hope you'd correct me if I'm wrong, you would not like to join the common run of lawyers to practise law in the courts for even the High Court is located in Simla, and commuting up and down will be rather forbiddingly strenuous.

'What I already had in my mind and surfaced after I had heard you is my chance meeting with Raja Hari Singh Thakur last weekend here, in the Circuit House, at a get-together. I thought he was fretting over the shoddy manner in which his legal advisor had been handling his matters pertaining to forest land and encroachments of some strongmen from villages around Kila Raipur, all of whom had mustered the strength of like-minded rebels to abet elements of lawlessness. The Raja is a mild-mannered peace-loving man who is proud of his library rather than his armoury. By some ingrained standard operating procedures, he expects others also to live by his upright standards. Maybe his thought process is not fit for the present time frame. The dark shadows of city culture have almost reached the chaste environs of the interiors of the area.

'Putting two and two together, without making it thirty-four' (both smiled) 'my suggestion is you and I make a trip to the state of Subathu to meet the Raja. I shall fix the time and day after I've talked with him sometime tomorrow morning. My hunch is, if nothing very untoward stands in the way, we shall land up at your destination. According to the tradition of the princely states, this kind of appointment is nothing short of handling a ministerial portfolio—you have independent charge of a department and will always be closest to the ruler himself for consultations. The personage is amply taken care of in return. The provision of appositely well-appointed living quarters with attendants, but the kitchen is run by the incumbent. Two Arabian-bred steeds, stable keepers and grooms all provided for. Give it a thought, Barrister. This is my idea and I see a good probability of it being accepted by the Raja Sahib. The decision and initiative have to be taken by you, the rest largely I shall take care of, but then, finally, all rests on the will of God.'

'You know, Nardev, you have read my mind better than any astrologer would have, and therefore, all the rest that you thought for me logically falls in place. There's hardly any space for gainsaying or thinking of ramifications. Thank you, indeed, for spending so much of your time to resolve my issue. I may have been even metaphorically preventing you from another drink. On my asking, therefore, let's have another to take our mind off the problem, which is no more a problem. Please, therefore, go ahead and fix the meeting and let's see how the outcome pans out. The human element in every situation is the most unpredictable part, though I'm sure whimsicality is the last human foible one would associate with a Raja of twenty-odd years of peaceful reign.'

'Oh yes, tomorrow, sometime towards the evening, I'll call you and tell you all. By then I should have had a word with the Raja, and will be able to offer you a piece of cake with your afternoon tea.' They laughed and were both happy, especially Nardev, because he thought he had been able to dispel the lines of anxiety off Vikram's brow. And Vikram was gratified by the assurance from Nardev that a veritable positive step had been taken in the direction of a desirable conclusion. He felt he was not wrong and had been intuitively guided to come and see Nardev. And here was some light at the end of a vexing dark tunnel.

They refilled their glasses. At the same time, considering the hands of the clock raced up to almost 9.30 p.m., Nardev got up and went inside. He whispered to Urmi to come out for a while and, like a good hostess, to keep the party going with her company for their business talk was over and also that she may tell the maid to lay the table. They would like to eat in another ten minutes, in spite of the savoury dumplings. Senior Mr Shastri was served dinner in his room as he liked it.

Vikram left Mr Nardev's lovely little cottage soon after ten. All went well and they were all in good cheer when

Vikram said good night to Nardev at the wicket gate and turned round to take a look at the small front garden, awash in silver in the moonlight.

Vikram was quite satisfied with the progress of the work on his own cottage and its annexe. He was of a mind and found time to call Ruby to give her the latest news about setting up the house. He knew it would go a long way to cheer her up. He was especially pleased with the outcome of his meeting with Nardev. The offer from Nardev to take up the matters thereon with the Raja of Subathu was more than he had expected. It just showed him that this world around us was not only peopled with screwy and shifty people, but one could take heart from essentially good human beings, adding pillars to stabilize their faith in life.

Nardev not only understood the difficulty in which he found Vikram, but offered to do all in his power to help the latter out because he felt he could; and found no reason why he should not. Most others in his place would have just kept quiet and looked the other way.

Come evening, around seven, there was a call from Nardev. His heart missed a beat when he heard that Nardev had talked with Raja Hari Singh of Subathu and that he had agreed to give Vikram Rana an audience. Besides, he would send his station wagon with the driver to fetch Nardev and his friend the day after, that is, Thursday morning. They should be on the road to Subathu by 9.30 a.m. Vikram thanked Nardev profusely for his effort to see to all possible options to get Vikram settled in a respectable job.

At Deoghat, about two miles from the Solan bus plaza,

leading up to Simla and beyond to Kinnaur and the border of Tibet, they turned left on the country road. It was not in a good state of repair. They headed through the Deobhoomi (the vales where gods dwell) towards the northwest. It was just about an hour's journey up to the main bus stop of Subathu, and another ten minutes to the Raja's palace at Kuthar, north-west of the huge shopping arcade around the bus station. The palace was, in fact, surrounded by broad parapet stone walls that went around the central fort area and a smattering of other residential buildings of the families of official staff of the Raja. The vistas were landscaped with ornamental plants, trees, a water channel and a tall fountain with a wide basin at the centre, all fed by a clear mountain rill.

They noticed a couple of road rollers in the midst of black clouds of coal tar, and so, the labourers too were sooty as they worked in the smoke and with molten tar. Busy carpeting and repairing the road, they were oblivious to the charm and opulence of the lush countryside with its terraced fields of crops of corn and the road winding around the bends of the slopes. Their royal blue and golden station wagon raised dust as it passed several tiny hamlets (each with its own bus stops and roadside shelters with strange sounding names) like Laghech, Matando and Kharpana; of these Matando was bigger than the others. There were more people waiting in the shelter of the bus stop and some vendors, too, with their fare of mixed fresh vegetables and fruits on small wheelbarrows. They lunged forward as the bus came to a stop there to find customers for their fare, each of which they called out by name. There were days when the sellers went back home happy, and there were times the young fellows with the wheelbarrows were not so lucky. They didn't mind it very much and romped back home with a devil-may-care attitude, with yapping and laughter, for it was that much less for their pocket money.

As Vikram and Nardev drove closer to Subathu, Vikram was struck by similar amazing names of the villages, but these clusters looked a bit more prosperous, with brick houses and slate-stone gabled roofs. Sometimes a smoking chimney too could be sighted at places like Kathni, Kaba Kalan and especially Kunihar or Kothi, closer to the township of Subathu. The driver took the last turn towards the palace from the main bus station, further northwest on the road winding through the lovely topography of knolls and dales, less than five miles from the turning at the bus station.

Hari Singh was of a tall healthy build and impressive bearing. The decor of his room was dominated by maroon satin and velvet; the metallic and wooden parts of the period furniture had a gold finish. The brass knockers and knobs on the doors were shining. The high roof of the morning room in which he welcomed his guests depicted battle scenes in a Mogul style of fine drawing—the perspective was in receding magnitude of figures, and not in terms of cold or warm colours, or the process of shading. He rose from his chair as the liveried guard opened the door and the two gentlemen walked in. His welcome smile was broad and warm as he shook hands with Nardev and Vikram, and Nardev gave a brief introduction of Vikram Rana. For refreshment, especially for the travellers, there was a wholesome bowl of mixed fruits and a carafe of home-brewed cider. The sallow-faced and erect butler poured their drinks and left the room in his dignified manner.

Hari Singh led his guests to their chairs and motioned them into their seats. The Raja then removed the lace serviette from the bowl and offered the fruit salad to his guests. And he said, 'I hope the journey was pleasant in spite of some bumpy patches on the road—where carpeting work is going on.'

A small introductory conversation led to Vikram dwelling at some length on his experiences in the law courts and some public events in the small town of Gujarat in West Punjab. This gave the Raja the opportunity to bring up the matter uppermost in his mind and to touch upon the matter that was the purpose of his guests' visit that morning. And he said, addressing himself primarily to Nardev who was familiar with the geography of the area, and for the benefit of Vikram who was going to be given the charge of tracking and undoing the crime network that, for some years now, had caused a variety of irritants for the Raja. He launched on, giving some details of the case to familiarize the prospective officer who was to deal with the whole situation on the ground. He went on to briefly recount the complexity of the situation, created especially by the involvement of persons of some political and social eminence in the social set-up of the villages, which were part of a well-knit network of local bodies of

Panchayats[2] to take care of the law and order under the state reporting rooms, directly under the Raja's cabinet within the Ministry of Internal Security.

Hari Singh gave them some description of the complications that had risen due to seizing the large area of borderland between the two villages. This contentious piece of land later had been made legal possession of the chief of the crime network, Hukumatrai. This was done through devious manoeuvres of the cunning and corrupt Patwari (a non-gazetted land officer with powers of land revenue collection and records of land demarcations). It was a huge task—penetrating the ring of criminals, maybe catching a malfeasant policeman's connivance, and also the sly support of a couple of embittered and sidelined ambitious politicians. The gigantic task would then require him, Vikram, to plan contra-moves for a long-run confrontation to contain and clip the wings of their wide-spanning area of strength and domination. He would finally restore the land to its rightful master, the Raja of Subathu.

The nefarious Hukumatrai Langda—the epithet 'Langda' was due to the limp in his stride caused by a nine-inch stag horn stilt for the lower part of his left leg that he had lost in a shootout with the state police—had had under him a faithful gang of eleven men, spread out in the neighbourhood villages, and they had terrorised not only Kunihar but also the neighbouring village, called Singhad Dwar, his own hideout

[2]A body of chosen representatives of the community like the jury. The body is headed by not a judge or a magistrate but by a leader known as the 'Sarpanch'.

with three of his confidantes. It was located somewhere among the natural grottos of the mountain range between the two villages.

Considering the impressive bearing of Vikram, being especially in awe of the power in his arresting blue eyes, his British degree of proficiency and competence at law, confirmed by the high recommendation of the experienced Nardev, whom the Raja had known and respected for more than two decades, the Raja had already made up his mind about giving a ministerial post to Vikram Rana, right among his trusted ministers.

Taking a look at his wristwatch, it was rather abruptly that Nardev stood up. He had been informed of the next engagement of the Raja's. He took a couple of steps towards Hari Singh with a genial smile and extended his hand to bid goodbye. The Raja took the opportunity to have a quick word with him. But Vikram was not quite out of earshot. He could partly overhear what passed between them, perhaps it was no more confidential. And then the Raja walked slightly towards Vikram as he said, 'I'm glad to learn about the forthcoming happy event in your life. So next when you come, we shall have the privilege of entertaining your gracious wife as well. In the meantime, let me convey to you my heartiest congratulations and wish you all the best. I can say it won't be very long before we'll see you and Mrs Rana back in Solan.'

Nardev took his cue and joined in, 'I, too, can only congratulate him for I am going to be busy along with you in the routine hearing of the matter of that land grabbing in the district court. Lala Hiralal has been duly subpoenaed and now there is no way that he can escape being present in the court. Indeed, I shall be looking forward to seeing him back here, not merely for his lively company.'

To this Vikram said, 'I'm a little dismayed that neither of you is joining to dance along with the baraatis in my loud Haryanvi marriage, or to gorge on the sumptuous dinner after the choicest of cocktails. And before parting, let me express my heartfelt thanks. To you, Raja Sahib, for arranging this lovely trip through the picturesque countryside. And indeed, the rich aromatic fresh cider was no less than ambrosia. Truly, I too shall look forward to seeing you.'

And he shot a sidelong glance at Nardev.

'I've sent for the driver with full instructions for your return journey.' Hardly were the words out of his mouth, when the station wagon came to a stop at the porch outside the main door. Nardev thanked his friend and shook hands with him. Following him, Vikram, too, said his goodbyes and shook hands with the Raja and they all began walking towards the gate.

'So I'll see you Monday morning any time after ten,' Nardev turned to the Raja and said, then began climbing down the steps after Vikram. They waved at one another, smiled and got into the waiting vehicle.

Within a couple of minutes, the car picked up its normal cruising speed and they were on their way back to Solan. It was then, in the privacy and quiet of the air-conditioned cabin, that Nardev went over what had passed between him and the Raja. The Raja, he told him, was a very intelligent man and from the brief little interjections of Vikram's—while he reviewed the tedious problem he was facing in his estates—he had made his own assessment of Vikram's intelligence and competence; especially by the questions he had asked about the movements of Langda's men, the kind of interference in the affairs of the people of the area, the role they played during the election (in tandem with the marginalised politicians of certain political parties). 'And by the time he came to the end of his version of the problem, he had made up his mind about inducting you into the administration of the state. In fact, he thought, to have a person of your education and intellectual calibre would be an asset to the staff of the government.'

Vikram was truly overwhelmed by the outcome of their visit to Subathu, which he had undertaken as a shot in the dark. Getting in touch with Nardev Shastri on a private hunch had turned out to be no less than a windfall. What made him truly glad was that the true worth of his competence had been valued and given due regard.

He couldn't reckon how to thank Nardev enough for all that he had thought and done for him. Because, ultimately, had Nardev not thought and done all that he did, such a tremendous achievement could merely have been an airy-fairy dream, like Cinderella's ball. Nardev gave direction to the driver to drop Vikram at the wicket gate entrance to his house, and then turned around and got back to the district courts, where his deputy was supposed to be waiting for him. The lunch hour drew close, and the Deputy took the precaution to postpone the matter due in the morning session to the post-lunch session. Within five minutes of reaching his office, his manservant Ramu brought his lunch in the customary hot case and went straight to his master's anteroom and left it there.

It was good that the Deputy was going back home for lunch instead of joining Nardev to eat lunch together as usual. He needed time alone to bring his mind to focus on the case, on which he had to hear the last part of the defence's argument and pass his order. Slowly and in peace, he ate his frugal mid-day meal, at the end of which he felt relaxed. He felt ready for the afternoon session.

As Vikram too began climbing the winding path to his house, his mind went back to Ruby, who he would make happy with the news of having landed the kind of job he most desired, where he would be placed in the kind of ambience that would suit his temperament. He was especially glad and grateful to God that his employer had given him the respect and esteem he deemed due to his status, going by his ancestry and the position that he was prospectively going to hold in the state of Subathu. Even calling up his father was secondary, to be done after he had talked to his sad, drooping Ruby, separated from him.

But his guilt choked him the moment he realised that he was not telling her the whole truth and how much pain he was going to cause his dearest one when, perhaps sheepishly, he would have to go like a schoolboy to a confessional to admit his first grave offence, his sin. Let all that come later, come with a trail of misery and suffering. But for now, he had to share with Ruby his great joy in its full impact and intensity.

The first thing he did, therefore, was to pick up the telephone and book a long-distance call for Ruby, via the Matron in charge of the labour room in Ford Hospital in Gujarat. He waited for her to come on the line. And after that, there was a period of choking words hurriedly blurted, overlapping one another, across the wires; there were sobs, tears and hiccups from both ends. Yet, considering the storm of emotions that she was labouring under, Vikram had to finally pour soothing oil over troubled waters to bring it all to an end with his assurance that, as things were shaping up, he was certain that the distance between them was not going to last long. Pacified for a while, Ruby talked to Vikram about the atmosphere in the city and the corridors of the hospital. It was charged with apprehension and, at times, there was a palpable fear of the looming vivisection of the country on communal lines. Vikram continued in the same vein and added to emphasise that this hardening of the political stand, which did not leave even Nehru unbitten by the bug (as his press conference indicated), had sealed the partition. Everybody seemed to be talking about the communally headstrong and polarised attitude of the Muslims and Hindus.

He hung up when Ruby had regained her poise after he had particularly urged her to convey his love and regards to her parents. The last words he said to her were his loving adjuration to not lose her good cheer and continue with her customary ardent prayers.

He had thought he would feel easy after putting down the receiver, just as his impression about Ruby was that she was quietened after he said all that to boost her morale—it would be of consolation to her. She did seem to have pulled herself together, but was not, he felt, in any kind of settled state of mind. On the contrary, he began to feel as though his conscience was swamped and writhing under a whole world cloaked in pretences and half-truths if not utter falsehoods. He began to wonder if the different versions of the truth, from different vantage points of his life, were a collage that formed the mosaic of a question mark, rather than a simple meaningful design.

This conundrum is what man must face as his predicament, and never be able to emerge triumphant from the maze of this chakravyuh! And instead of skill and valour in battle, which only Prince Arjun had, as the *Mahabharata* reveals, man today must resort to the cunning of the wicked. He must be prepared with an adequate variety of masks and shifty moves to beat the deceptive hologram of life. He must learn to master the art of a life of deception and act out a multitude of parts at a moment's notice. One really couldn't claim to be truthful, even to one's own self; how could one then be truthful to the next one? It was, indeed, difficult to put a finger on which is your true self. For in every condition, in the flux of life, the self and, accordingly, the masked appearance is changed to play the part. You are undecided about whether the reality at this moment or the reality a moment ago was true. This life is no less than living among the shifting images of a moving dystopian world.

Vikram's mind gushed with the memories from the past. And so one day as life seemed moving smoothly in its grooves—Vikram, while in Sonepat, was visiting a family friend, a retired doctor, Colonel Ghosh, if only for the sake of being in the company of the charming, doe-eyed and amiably inclined Mrs Shubhra Ghosh. Mrs Ghosh who, from her body language, he thought was more than just nice and friendly. Self-conscious, she seemed to make every movement studied to a certain effect. The welcome hug she gave him, he felt, was closer and with slightly more pressure than to the liking or social tolerance of watchful bystanders. Neither was there anything suggestive or lascivious, nor did the intent reflect any trace of blemish in any of her movements; unless she, very deftly like a skilled actress, camouflaged it. Except, as he happened to notice once or twice, her beautiful brown naughty eyes had the ability to pause for a lengthened moment and ogle at whoever she thought stood out for her special attention and admiration. Later, she created time and occasion to get closer to the he-man and strike up an idle conversation. And so, he felt her actions may have been easily taken for being bold and close to nudging the borders of moral impropriety, even when she was in a polite conversation in a first-time chance meeting with an unknown but comely stranger. Some could even go away with the impression that being a senior officer's wife gave her the licence of such freedom and placed her beyond blame. The fact, he learnt later, was that she made use of such a licence especially when her husband was posted out and she stayed in town for her daughter's education.

In her reckless tomcatting, she sometimes found herself pitched among riff-raff. Regret, if at all, when sanity restored itself, was short-lived. Until, incorrigibly, such next encounter. Sometimes whim-impelled, she'd sit in the car's front seat alongside the young driver. Her nonchalant swagger, more an attitude of a shallow mind, remained inveterately disabused. Wagging tongues ceaselessly spin yarns, and Vikram sifted and gathered from it all that she even flew long distances to gratify her craving itch. The material gain was never absent from the predatory sidelong glances she gave away. Her delicate feminine charms disguised a hard-nosed bargainer. This, perhaps, had settled in her character—to be part of a family and yet manage to gallivant in the face of domestic snarls—as a habit now. Another good friend of hers inadvertently confided that she could perceptibly notice the change in Mrs Ghosh's voice, which rose like a bird freed from its cage in flight into open skies before she boarded her flight. She had called her from the waiting lounge at the airport. These, and such others, were things Vikram had heard as tell-tales about her making rounds, among friends and family, and the focal point of interest always turned out to be some rich and wanton licentious society bird out there. She was branded a predator.

It was just salacious scandal-mongering of some sick minds, but it sounded quite unbelievable and sickening in the context of someone he respected. Somewhere, it outraged a privately-nourished and adored image of Shubhra in his heart. And, indeed, it took some time before things got sorted and settled in his mind, and he was quiet. For whenever he had met Shubhra, and he really looked forward to seeing her, he met her like his very first meeting, with a peculiar thrill of joy. As they say, the cockles of his heart were tickled in her presence.

On that particular evening, the family were going to the Cantonment Club for a celebration ball and dinner, and Shubhra had invited him to join the event as her personal friend—not to the liking of her mother-in-law, whose brow was defined in a definite scowl. In a short while, Vikram noticed that Shubhra was slightly tipsy even before the evening began in earnest at the club with a toast of champagne. In her sardonic sense of humour, it seemed, she enjoyed leaving people who had the cheek to raise eyebrows at her behaviour cheesed off in a helpless huff. She seemed to gloat within herself in the triumph of a battle of wits.

She left Vikram in her husband's company, saying, 'I'm sure you'd enjoy his company listening to his account of the action he witnessed during the war on the eastern front, in the slushy terrain of Malaya and the East Indies. I'll be back in a moment.'

Once again, he saw the naughty smile lighting up her eyes. In about an hour's time, when she returned to the table, they had been joined by mutual friends, Brigadier and Mrs J.M. Vora, lately retired from the Royal Indian Army, Imperial Defence of India. But Vikram truly had enjoyed the vicarious thrills as he listened to Dr Ghosh's narrative of reconstruction—almost live vignettes comprising anecdotes based on first-hand experiences when he was managing the medical service camp behind heavy artillery on the front during the last year of his active service.

There was an extra flush on Shubhra's face, and the white

of her eyes showed protuberant red arteries. She smiled and greeted the Voras, and was relieved to find the doctor engaged deeply in discussing the problem of high cholesterol with Vora, who had complaints related to it. She found the opportunity to walk over to Vikram's side of the table and drew an unoccupied chair from an adjacent table, and sat down close to him. Both were happy. He liked her, and she found an escape in his company. A couple more drinks in which she allowed herself to indulge loosened her tongue. It always happened. Her feminine loquacity began to manifest and irrevocably took hold of her.

'My journalist friend, Mrs Choudhury, shared a shocking story with me about a prominent political leader. Despite projecting an image of upstanding character, she uncovered evidence suggesting he was running a ring that provided easy access to young and ambitious women who were willing to exchange their favours for political gains,' she told Vikram.

Vikram, who had been wary of gossip, found himself agreeing with Mrs Choudhury's assessment. He pondered whether the leader's actions were driven by greed, a lust for power or an insatiable desire for sexual pleasure. Whatever the reason, it was clear that these women were being exploited and forced to compromise their integrity for the promise of advancement on the social ladder.

Vikram expressed his sympathy for the women involved, acknowledging that they likely felt guilt and shame for their actions. He couldn't help but feel disgusted by the leader's behaviour, which he likened to that of a pimp. It was a sordid tale of exploitation and immorality that left him deeply troubled.

Vikram would always wonder how it was possible for someone like Shubhra to contain and smother the emotions that must have churned and churned within her and for how long—until perhaps the stopper had reached its ultimate strength of preventing a blow-up. She hunched and almost turned her back towards the Voras and her husband's ongoing exposition on cholesterol, and with her eyes brimming with tears, she could hardly blurt out—'I am one! Vikram, you don't know how cruel the world is. Everything, even a human being, is treated like a chucked commodity, which is stapled with a price tag. And nothing, just nothing, can be done without paying the costs.'

She brought out her handkerchief from her handbag to cover her nose and eyes and, for a moment, let herself go. She was though able to pull herself together in a few minutes, before attracting anybody's serious notice in the loud cacophony of people drinking and making conversation with one another.

'I can take care of myself,' she said as she shook off Vikram's hand, who had tried to take her by the hand and lead her to the washroom. With her handkerchief still covering her nose with one hand, she briskly walked towards the toilets. After a few hesitant steps, Vikram thought it proper to return to his seat. And when Dr Ghosh saw him alone and not in the company of his wife, he queried, more by signal, raising his eyebrows, and added, 'Where's she?'

Pointing with his thumb to the alleyway leading to the

toilets, he said shortly, 'Washroom.'

Given to authoritative presumption, the doctor said with a smirk, 'During a party, she gives herself the liberty of indulging in a drop too much. She's okay, though?'

'Oh yes, she's fine,' he assured the doctor and settled down in his chair. The doctor took up the line of exposition where he'd left off, and Vora got easily engrossed in continuing with it. With one surreptitious look at his wristwatch, Ghosh suggested that they hurry up with their dinner and return home. He was worried about his eighty-year-old mother alone at home with the attendant maid. The parting was a bit too sombre for Vikram's liking. He was anguished by the kind of misery he saw Shubhra going through before she could hold no more and broke down. He, therefore, tried to leave her with a reassuring note as he parted and said good night.

'I'll come to see you tomorrow. Maybe we can go out for a cup of tea to the Nuggets for your favourite muffins.'

'Welcome any time,' she said.

The present is so prepossessing, Vikram's emotions swung along and changed direction and kept pace with the highs and lows of the experience of the evening. Besides, he had gotten to know Mr Vora more closely and liked his warm amiability. He found him quite different from the usual slightly stiff-necked men in the political scene.

He returned to his room and his bed with a choking emotion, the cause of which was the deeply touching episode of Shubhra's outburst, which for some time shook him for several reasons. It brought into focus the depressing variety of her conjugal relationship. And now, for a long time, he couldn't fall asleep. Like a view from the wrong end of a telescope, images of his past life, of London days, started flitting across his mind—a metaphor to sum up the image of his climbing the flight of stairs up to his hostel room in the wee hours of a morning. He clearly saw his cadaverous face, totally weary and depleted from heavy drinking, and how physically, mentally and spiritually miserable he was. He was then a wretched debauch, having lost the last penny of the pocket money he was allowed. The kaleidoscopic turn shifted the scene to meeting his father at the station and then the credulous members of the family at home, who left him utterly bamboozled by the shuffling of events and the moral considerations he had created for himself.

And thus, going back and forth over such images, he didn't know when he lost the train of thought and drifted into a shallow sleep.

He woke up in the morning with his still heavy head, and confused thoughts and memories of dreams during a badly slept night. Freshness was nowhere to be seen. He took rather long, lazing in bed, before he pushed himself out of it and went through the motions of his habitual morning routine like a wound but a rusted automaton. He began to undo the warped ball of thoughts and the yarn of the night's memories in his head. In a very short while, he flung his arms and gave up, as perhaps the first philosopher may have done while looking at the paradoxes of life to ponder and resolve in search of the design and, if at all, the designer of it all.

The greatest paradox, Vikram found, was his own life—the order and yet containing chaos. He had just allowed himself to drift along with the current of circumstance and situation in which his life's unfolding time had placed him. The driving force of his volition was indeed there—the clear and firm set of values imbibed in his rearing. But it seemed to him that there was something more than compelling about the elemental force in man that overrode the best values on man's part to counter and break what judgement may decide was best to be left alone to triumph or capitulate. Most times, he thought, it was after the event, after the typhoon had blown over, leaving a trail of devastation in its wake, that the dawn of wisdom breaks, too late for any amends, except for volitional endeavours for atonement and the purgatory of waiting for true justice. The justice reached via rungs of five imperfect senses, added with that of their most refined part, the rational mind, is bound to be wanting. Yet, facing the harsh imperfect existential reality still remains the best option for man, more than any simulated utopia. The paradigm of life may be altered at the ground level; so be it. There will be plenty of ongoing moral skirmishes at the subterranean level, which like a drag must be, like Sisyphus, pushed along the climb all life.

And so along the drift, he was again going to allow himself, almost wilfully, to be drawn into the dreaded whirlpool, for it was indeed unthinkable for him to defy his father and the whole world of his rearing in the family. He had done that once before and found himself living in a miry world of tumbling half-truths, deceptions and outright falsehood. Images overlapped images, flitting by before the eyes could focus, and the truth of an event remained ever undiscovered, lost like a needle in a haystack.

Such were his dreams. They ended with him being chased by a firm-jawed jaguar through a tangled bushy forest. Treading in hesitant steps, with bravado nevertheless, towards the staircase leading up to a winding corridor along the inviting cabins, showcasing objects of pleasure. It all came back to his mind. Trampled and crushed under the tread of his sole came the rigmarole of flitting images; added to the rest was the stunning memory of the party last night, the bubble that blew like a bomb. His dejected head was weighed down with the baggage of guilt and helplessness in the face of the inevitability of the flux of the events of life.

He was yet goaded on by his duty to get along and do his best to what in his judgement was right. So early the next day, he called on his friend, Nardev, to let him know how grateful he was for settling his future life in Solan. And that he would be leaving for home that very afternoon by the roadways bus leaving at half past one, after a quick lunch. He hoped to see him soon, to be together in good times.

11

Vikram Rana's journey turned out to be long and circuitous before he and his family were settled as one of the few eminent families in Solan. They had the respect of social status due to Vikram Rana's close connection with the Royal House of Subathu, his education and as his two elder sons were resident students in Lahore Government College, and because of their lifestyle. The stretched span of time took within its ambit two historic events that radically changed a number of things (overtly as well as subtly) in the life of the Ranas at home in Sonepat and later in their new home at Solan.

One of the two was evidently the imminent marriage for which the preparations in his family had been in progress for some time now, and Vikram cowered in guilt.

Yet, as his father knew, he had dared himself to take the plunge. The ceremonies of the conjugal union were in the horrid shadow of the other event, which darkened under its cover a very large mass of the population. The migrations were ongoing. The scourge of the country's cursed partition, which was geographically depicted on the newly published maps of the country, the land mass of India, was merely a parochial satisfaction of political egos. The damage that made inroads into the collective communal psyche was a polarization that resulted from religious indoctrination.

Other fanatical communal leaders, preaching bigotry and staunch religious and political concepts and ideas, joined the campaign to penetrate and influence pockets of the gullible polity. Their whirlwind of untenable ideas spread like wildfire; and forever, like canker, was embedded into the very mindset of the unthinking and vulnerable. Thus, stronger and taller than any concrete walls, the wall of hostility and hatred was raised. The British rulers, with a smirk, put a price on the problem of granting political freedom to India and were relieved to have the monkey off their back.

The pain from vivisection was present in another small corner in the town of Gujarat in West Punjab, and overwhelmed it in its sweeping billow of the sedate Christian family of Father Constantine.

And yet, for a while, Ruby had no apprehension whatsoever of the ominous havoc, worse than the more pervasive one that hung on the horizon of her nascent little world. Her fervent heart was still young and tender. It wasn't ready yet for the advancing, distant celestial rumble that would later materialize in fierce turbulence. Both her parents, aware of the crowding national calamity and cowed by dark apprehensions, went about with grim and drawn faces. They avoided deliberately touching upon the topic of the time that was elapsing—weeks into months and months into years.

And though Ruby did hear from Vikram, his calls were fewer and far between, and they filled her heart with doubts and fears. These she always waived off by means of the faith she had in her very own Vikram.

Alva tried her best to find more and more time to spend with her child to share with her the weight of her heart full of concerns. She tried to engage Ruby in the conversation of things mundane, trying her best to bring up the topic of news from Vikram. And most of the information she could gather from Ruby's conversations was that things were good, except that she did not know when he would come to fetch Ruby into her new home, as he had hinted at it several times while calling, or in his letters. But these were now becoming frightfully less frequent. She tried her best to explain this circumstance, attributing it to every kind of pretext she could invent for herself and her mother.

So the things stood at her end or rather crawled alongside the drudging duty hours at the hospital. Patiently bearing with hard times and taking on the share of pain that passage brings. It is true that braving adversities strengthens the fibre of endurance in character. Ruby seemed to be learning the lesson the hard way. That she did not flinch and with her faith firmly in place in her heart, especially in the veracity of all that Vikram stood for, she strode along with the adjuration, 'The Lord walks with one who walks alone', in her eyes against all adverse winds. It was going to stand her in good stead and provide her with a shield and shelter during rainy days. Buttressed with such faith, she began preparing, even if it were for a long haul; for intuitively, she saw the circumstances developing to indicate such conditions. Time for her, it seemed, would continue dragging its feet.

Ruby had waited for twenty long years before finally deciding to come to Solan, a place she now called her own. She spotted a few grey hairs in her shiny long black tresses before her life's earnest beginning was ushered in, in time's stride after two decades or so. However, upon arriving, she was taken aback by the fact that Vikram, whom she had been in contact with, had a full-fledged family with a wife and four children.

Vikram had kept Ruby updated on the developments in his life, but she was not fully prepared for what she was about to face. He had warned her that the changes in his life would affect her as well and that she would have to mentally prepare herself to become a part of his extended family.

Although Ruby had anticipated the situation, she was still apprehensive and felt overwhelmed. It was almost like facing a double-edged sword, where the changes could have both positive and negative consequences. Nonetheless, Ruby had made the decision to come to Solan, and she was determined to make the best of it.

Yet she seemed to have taken courage from the fact that it was her husband, her very own Vikram, who had first 'phoned' and then 'written' to urge her to come over. It was her journey back home, although a mite too late; still, she was coming home to her husband, who cared for her as ever, and she must never allow the feeling of being a stranger to assail her mind. The icing on the cake was that he had sent a first-class rail ticket for her journey throughout, with an amount of five thousand rupees for sundry expenses. Her heart felt buoyed with more assurance still when she found the youngest of the Ranas, Premchand, on the platform to receive her as Mr Rana, which he hastened to inform her—he addressed her as aunty, quite spontaneously in a fluster—was at work in Subathu, detained by something urgent and important, and would hurry back to meet her around two in the afternoon.

Premchand had a broad and candid smile on his slightly bony face. His fair skin was covered with a shade of teenage downy growth, which immediately caught Ruby's attention. She noticed that Vikram's face flickered in Premchand's, particularly the cut and twinkle of his eyes as he talked. This helped Ruby overcome her initial hesitation and start talking to Premchand in a warm, free and affectionate tone.

Vikram seemed to have moved on from his past in Gujarat, but Ruby couldn't. The friendly and welcoming nature of Premchand reminded her of Vikram in his old days in Gujarat. Although he appeared hesitant at first, he quickly shed his inhibitions and engaged in conversation with Ruby.

Ruby, in contrast, was unable to move beyond her past experiences. Her previous traumas still burdened her, and her encounters with new people were marked by fear and suspicion. Despite the warmth and friendliness of Premchand, she could not help but be guarded around him, viewing him through the lens of her past experiences.

It seemed to her more amazing than a sea change when she found herself surrounded by hills all around, a very clean, bracing cool air to breathe—things she hadn't noticed during the time she spent on the bus or train. Her mind, time and again, went back to imagining the uncertain family situation she was going to face at her destination to notice and dwell over the beauty of scenic changes at every turn, several assurances of Vikram nevertheless. She trembled slightly, but tangibly, with the thought of being an intruder or arriving as an outsider into the peaceful family ambience. Indeed, the smaller and slower train did impress her as amusing, like footage of a cinema film, though she was fascinated by the sight of the greenery of hillsides and pine forests.

The one porter that Premchand had engaged was enough to carry the few pieces of luggage. He strapped the suitcases and carried the baskets, and began to exit the platform speedily. He went ahead and climbed the winding stairs up to the main road, which they had to cross to reach the wicket gate of entry to the Rana Estate. To have been given the very name of the place was enough for him to carry the luggage and reach the well-known Rana Cottage before Ruby, chaperoned by Premchand, slogged their way up. Ruby felt slightly short of breath by the time they reached the house past the annexe, where all arrangements for Ruby's stay had been made. The well-appointed two-bedroom apartment on the first floor had been particularly readied under Vikram's personal supervision. She was to be put up there for the course of time, during which she would get familiar with the family.

Vidya had been aware of her responsibility of integrating Ruby into the family, as Vikram had made sure to indoctrinate her on the matter. She had mentally prepared herself for this task and had even dropped hints to her elder children, Omdutt and Vidyadhar, about the arrival of a new family member, so that it wouldn't come as a shock to them. However, despite her preparations, Vidya felt a great deal of sorrow that she couldn't show. She was worried about how Ruby would fit in and whether or not the family would accept her. She was also concerned about the effect that Ruby's arrival would have on her youngest son Premchand.

Despite these concerns, Vidya was determined to make Ruby feel welcome. She recognized that it was largely her responsibility to ensure that the merger between Ruby and the rest of the family went smoothly. Vidya was a highly intelligent and knowledgeable woman, and her relationship with her husband was multifaceted, involving long horse rides into the hills. Her youngest son, Premchand, was particularly fond of her and would frequently go on outings with her. Overall, Vidya was doing her best to navigate the complexities of welcoming a new family member, even as she struggled with her own doubts and fears.

Today, Divya was all aflutter since morning, for her father had broken the news to her about going back to Solan by midday. The special occasion was to receive and meet the aunt who her father, by way of introducing her, had been giving Divya information about in snatches, adopting a generally convivial tone and manner of typical bantering to avoid giving her any unpleasant surprise at what led to the arrival of an aunt from a distant part of the subcontinent, and from a time before her birth. She was now going to meet her face to face and, perhaps, live in her company in times to come. She felt queered when she tried to imagine that this woman was a part of the family far more deeply than anyone was ready to admit—she belonged to her own father's earlier days of his job in what was now Pakistan. And on the grounds of the stray facts of information, she was able to visualise how the lady, too, had her parents attached to one another and were long concerned about when their daughter would go to live with her husband. Her father, she was sure, must have told them the truth about the circumstantial changes his life had gone through with the passage of time. And therefore, though rather late in the day, he had maintained the firm line of his integrity and had called her to give her place of respect and dignity in the family. She felt proud of her father and breathed deeply to put a stop to her nervous fluster. She felt better and was ready to accompany her father to meet and, yes, welcome the new, though late, entrant to the family.

After a brief repast of a bowl of mixed fruits, father and daughter took their seats in the station wagon, one of the two cars allocated for Rana Sahib's personal use. The chauffeur put the car in gear and moved out of the premise of the residential area. Soon he was on his way to Solan.

Having completed her round of the mandi area where Vidya had to get some urgently needed provisions, she took the shortcut to turn into the sabzi mandi for fresh vegetables and fruits. The midday sun was getting warmer when she decided to get back home to receive and meet her important guest. Over the previous weeks, whenever they had been able to spend time together, on the weekends mostly, Vikram had been giving her the necessary high points of the events of his past and about his relationship with Ruby and her family during his first posting in Gujarat, now in Pakistan. He depended upon Vidya's strong sense of propriety to deal with the two elder boys, Omdutt and Vidyadhar, whereas he managed the youngest Premchand, for he, after having dropped out of school and wriggled across matriculation, had been spending most of his time with his father in Subathu, where he had descended on the streets of the town and neighbourhood with an advantage of his father's renown of authority and influence beyond office and administration.

He had created his own infamous domain of influence as far as he drove his father's black Baby Austin on the country roads to villages of near distances. Having taken after his father in several physical aspects, he struck a chord of awe among people wherever he went. It was not long for him to recognise his own power of presence among commonalty. Taking advantage of such a situation, and presuming his reputation had reached his father by hearsay, he made an outrageous proposition to his father.

'I'm sure, sir, you are aware of the fact that there is always a dearth of taxis plying between the railway junctions of Kalka and Simla. There's a jostling crowd always trying to get a taxi or just a seat in one. A loud melee is created around the few taxis at the Stand. It should be a good idea to start using our car as a taxi for the few busy hours of the morning, and maybe make one trip in the evening, when possible, to cater to the passengers aiming to take the last train to Delhi or Calcutta. I can take the responsibility to get the paperwork done and take care of the rest of the hassles. I'm sure you can depend on me. Father?'

'This nonchalance...,' Vikram said, '...on your part about the enterprise of a substantial investment, I hope, is no mere flippancy, but reflects a true spirit of your confidence. Indeed, on second thought, you could make it work, but I can allow you the use and maintenance of the car only for a month. And I can put aside a fixed amount of money for your emergency use. We, that is, you and I, will take stock of the situation after a month of an accident-free trial. The money I didn't spend on your education will be your financial support in the transport business.'

Vikram didn't let go, he smiled, which was more of a smirk, and added, 'The rider to this arrangement, the important part of mutual understanding is that we'll fix the trial period for six months (from the day you carry your first fare from Kalka to Simla). And during that period, you shall pay fifty per cent of the maintenance and fuel expenses. You shall then hand over the car to me in perfectly fit and running condition and after that apply for a loan from a bank for the purchase of a motor vehicle to run as a taxi. I shall stand surety in your favour for the loan and the monthly instalment. It is entirely your responsibility to be answerable for everything in the agreement of the loan application. You must, in advance, make sure and then promise me of it before I sign the contract papers with the bank that there would be earnings enough every month to redeem the instalments after you have paid for the fuel and maintenance of the car.' The father's face remained stern for a while and then relaxed. Vikram's intention was not to frighten his son but to drive home to him the seriousness of the whole business of dealing with the bank. It was different from dealing with his father. The law takes over the moment any irregularity or lapse is discovered in the account books.

Premchand remained stupefied for a while and then, a bit hesitatingly and with white-faced bravado, said, 'The six months you give for trial should be time enough for me to judge if I can take the plunge. I, too, wouldn't wish to push you into any kind of embarrassing situation for a no-good son.'

Things were left at that until Premchand could come up with an auspicious date on which to break a consecrated coconut to launch the family car as a taxi on the Kalka–Simla route, busy with tourists and holidaymakers during summers from the whole length and breadth of the country. It was just like in the Kashmir Valley, where the tourists flock in all seasons, not only for its breathtaking scenic landscapes and lakes but also for the variety of luscious fruits that amaze you with their colours and flavours around the year. And this keeps the land routes, waterways and airways busy; a major part of the commerce in Kashmir is from tourism and ancillary vocations and industries.

So it was as though Premchand, at this juncture, stood poised on the edge of a springboard of his own decision and volition. He was prepared to take the plunge into his dream adventure. Higher education and academics, he had long come to the conclusion, were beyond his abilities or inclination. To his father, though, who had had the privilege of holding important offices that provided him with the luxury of aristocratic life, it was something of an ambitious enterprise for a callow and inexperienced youth. The uncharted waters of the transport business were infamously known to be infested with sharks. And indeed, Premchand had had a vicarious taste, if not the experience of the muddied rapids of crime and intrigue of devious politicians and violent criminals of the countryside from the stories he had heard from his father. He, therefore, had made up his mind to explore an independent vocation, rather than the easier, pedestrian, beaten path of joining a petty job in the state government or some flourishing business concern, where one always had to look up to his seniors and keep them pleased. There seemed to be, inherently, a tendency to dream big and a will strong enough to pursue his ambitious vision and to give it all he had. Sparsely equipped with intellectual or academic competence, his confidence goaded him on to give it a fling in right earnest and make it good in the end, maybe.

Vidya was a regular visitor to the bustling Ganj Market, also known as the Central Market, accompanied by Mastram, for her weekly supply of fresh produce. After purchasing her preferred selection of seasonal fruits and vegetables, she headed back home with plenty of time to prepare her signature dishes. Today, her mind was occupied with thoughts of two special guests who would be joining her for lunch. Her husband was returning from Subathu after a week, cutting short a crucial meeting with the Raja to be at home to welcome Ruby, who was finally coming back to her beloved home. Vidya pondered over what to cook for this joyous occasion, eager to impress her guests with her culinary prowess.

Meanwhile, Vidya's mind wandered back to the tranquil days spent in Subathu as she accompanied Vikram to their residential bungalow allocated to him by Hari Singh. The scenic beauty of the place was etched in her memory—the lush greenery, wooded hillsides and occasional sighting of the larger cats, such as cheetahs, foxes and hyenas, that roamed the jungles.

The bungalow was well-appointed, with a staff of attendants and servants at their beck and call. It had become a second home for the family, offering a peaceful escape from the hustle and bustle of the city. However, except for Premchand, neither of the other two boys had ever stayed there for an extended period. They preferred to visit during short holidays or weekends to indulge in their interests, such as fishing or shooting wild fowl, pheasant and hare in the interior of the wooded hillsides.

As Vidya reminisced about Subathu, she could almost feel the cool breeze blowing through her hair and the serenity of the place washing over her. It was a picturesque town that had captured her heart, and even now, years later, the memories of their time there still brought a smile to her face.

One characteristic of her husband, which Vidya had got to know fairly well by now, was that he was a very methodical man and hardly ever veered away from his prioritized schedules. Even the two drinks that he had as an appetiser before dinner, he got poured at half past seven without variation. He spaced them so that he was at the dinner table at half past eight. Yet she wondered with so much else coursing through her mind as she walked back home after her list of purchases that morning that there was something, quite an unfathomable pressure, for Vikram to truncate the matter with the Raja to come away to receive and be with Ruby in good time.

In such emotional matters, Divya seemed to be empathetically more sensitive and was stirred by the ineffable vibrations of her father, and she was at her father's side all the way through. In contrast, Vidya, in her thoughts involving the pros and cons of the situation she found herself in, still remained overwrought by restrictive consideration of traditional constraints.

After a great deal of Vikram's effort at chiselling and shaping the sharps and flats, he felt satisfied that Vidya's hostility was grounded in her having been reared in family circles governed largely by orthodox values. Indeed, there were several instances of polygamy and even polyandry, maybe infrequent, in society. Not having to go far for example, Vikram had cited the event in his own family—though it was never meant as a pretext, but hoping that awareness can lead to tolerance. And he had a perception of such a widening of horizon in Vidya's mind.

Or was it a wishful thought? For she reverted back and forth to the criss-crossing thoughts in her mind, thoughts at cross purposes with one another. She could not be negatively inclined because of the essential goodness of temperament in her. Hers was not a morbid mind. Apparently, there was indeed no reason she could find to condone having a stranger under her roof, she thought, and to share her husband's care and attention, if not love as well. And, as counter, she could not but grant and so accept the fact that Ruby, whom she again and again thought of as a stranger, was the one who had first claimed, and for which she had, without a squeak of complaint, stoically lived a forced monastic life.

And now she had come, not on the strength of rightful and even legal reclamation, but almost like one dithering to seek favour, with the support of the ruling power of the family nevertheless. Vidya's essential goodness and her good sense of reason, as also her awareness of the ground reality, kept her long on the see-saw of turmoil as she made her way through the winding narrow streets of Solan and headed for home. She had, for a fleeting moment, been able to get into Ruby's shoes in passing. And so by the time she climbed the last few steps up into her home, she had a small smile playing around her face, free of lines of worry.

And wonderfully she found herself thinking of receiving Ruby as a member of Vikram's family. For as the last word of a jumble of thoughts was that, had it not been for the circumstances not indeed of her creation, the whole scenario would have been quite different. And so, too, what emerged was, yes, she rightfully was a member of the family. In fact, she thought, it was incumbent upon her that she should see to it that for Ruby, in ample measure, things must be made up for. She had been through a gruelling tussle with adversity, and she was driven into it for no fault of hers. Vidya would do her utmost to apply whatever would work like a balm to alleviate Ruby's festering wounds.

The few stray clouds that had darkened the morning sky had drifted away. There was bright sunshine, and a refreshing cool breeze had sprung up, laden with a pine aroma as she sat down in the living room, admiring afresh the sights of hills and downs from her windows. She waited for guests arriving from Subathu, and also a long way from down in the plains after a long and tiresome journey. The south-west monsoon had receded by the end of September from the mountains, leaving their laps with ample blessings until the next year. The October skies were clear and bright blue. The valleys in the light of the setting sun were filled with a veritable pink mist.

Parvati, the young daughter of Mastram, had replenished the flower vases with fresh flowers. Under the guidance of her mistress, Parvati had learnt to be an accomplished posies maker. With her mind and heart having shed their passions, and no worry gnawing at her, Vidya basked in her domestic bliss and thanked her deity for the rare moment of tranquillity that had descended upon her soul. And in that moment, she thought of her Bua with gratitude. She brought her round to choosing the life of marriage when it was being offered to her on a platter, and when an exigency caused by some quirk of fate came along, she had garnered experience. And with experience came the quiet strength to take it on, without allowing the stability of life of the family to be disturbed. She had the strength to turn to what commonly might have been considered a calamity of sorts, into an opportunity, to make a sacrifice and improve the health of the family. She had imparted a sense of better mutual understanding and homogeneity among the children, and thus, won over not only the approbation of her most loved and adulated one but infused goodwill among all members. The message, by indirection, was also to point out how important this was for the happy state of the family. The pain of sacrifice is the price necessary to pay for obtaining peace and harmony in the family.

The gong at the railway station was struck, and it could be heard over at the Rana House. It was the announcement that the first Kalka–Simla train had arrived on the platform. Vidya was alerted to come out of her state of languor and get ready for the last-minute preparations to receive her first guest.

She called out to Mastram to give him his set of instructions and went round the rooms for one last look before she thought she could take Ruby round the house to show her the premises. She was well satisfied with the set-up of the annexe living quarters that had been readied for Ruby. She had taken her last look of approval on her way to the market in the morning and okayed it. Fifteen minutes from the time of arrival of the train, Premchand would be up home, along with his stepmother.

It was a climb all the way—first the cement stairway from

the platform, up to the main road and across the road, the winding climb from the wicket gate of entry to the estate, then to the house. Besides, Ruby was not accustomed to hillside climbing and so they might take more time than what Premchand would have usually taken.

The formality of their first meeting was subdued by Vidya's genuine warmth and her welcome smile as she put her arm around Ruby's shoulders in a hesitant semi-embrace and led her to a comfortable and cushioned cane chair in the living room. A tablecloth embroidered with the cheerful colours of autumn flowering was spread over the small round table, which was laid with coffee things.

'You must be tired after the long journey and feeling a bit down. You've come a long way away, separated from your parents, yet must be sanguine about meeting Vikram and the newly formed family.'

'Oh yes, how true you are! Every limb of mine is aching and I'm feeling so utterly limp and lifeless. Believe me, it's just because of these very two reasons. But you, being so considerate, and your warm cordiality have indeed taken the edge off all my fatigue. And yes, Vikram had written to me about the welcome I shall receive in the family. It has been an emotional crutch throughout. The affability of the young man, Premchand, whom you so generously sent to receive me at the station; his warm winsome smile, in a moment, rid me of the stiff nervous state in which my heart screeched as the train pulled up at the station. I don't know how he located me and began talking to me, as though we knew each other for ages.'

Premchand, who had just emerged from the toilet, joined the ladies and smiled with a blush on having heard the last bit of what Ruby had been saying to Vidya.

'Oh, Ruby aunty, you know, Father had been telling me a lot about you. I alone spend most of my time with him there in Subathu. Of late, though, since we came to know of your coming over to join us, I was hopefully waiting for you to join me and father for some long stretches of time so I could take you out on horse rides to discover and enjoy the largely green and colourful spots of rocky primaeval beauty of this densely wooded hinterland part of the town. Mommy here is fond of the life in town and is happy to be part of the groovy social life in the company of the wives of other civil and army officers stationed in Solan. But before she despatched me to the station to be there as the one-man reception committee for you—the two older brothers were not available and will be back at home from Simla only after four in the afternoon when their work in the district courts comes to an end for the day—Mom was particular that I was properly indoctrinated about the whole situation. She takes me for a kid still, even though she knows I've lived under my father's wings for the longest period of time. It is my education and training period in the Gurukul.' He then permitted himself to indulge in a broad and knowing smile.

Vidya joined in and said, 'It is not in his character though, but Vikram seemed to have dithered too long before he began to open up about you. And reminiscing, told me about the evening in the Gujarat club when he first met you. And then, how soon your mom gathered him in her familial arms to make him a part of your family. Not stopping there, he told me how difficult it was for him to tear himself away from you after just a short while on receipt of an urgent letter from his father. I must admit to you that, much above everything else, I admire his honesty and abiding truthfulness in his allegiances. Let me, therefore, put you at your ease and assure you that you are as much a part of this family as he has been yours since then in Gujarat.'

Pushing her chair backwards, Ruby got up abruptly as though reminded of something in particular. 'Excuse me a moment,' she said and disappeared into the adjacent room where her luggage had been deposited and returned with a heavy cane basket covered with a large floral napkin stitched down. She continued, 'Here are some fruits and sweets, along with a plum cake, which my mother specially baked for the family. Vikram was totally bowled over by Mama's plum cake when he first tasted it on Christmas.'

'O, how sweet of her to have thought of us and sent the gifts that you have brought. Let me share your time when you call your parents. I'd like to thank her personally; I'm so overwhelmed, truly.'

'I'll do that, surely. It will only be after I've showered and settled down.'

'By then I hope Vikram will arrive, and maybe he too would like to have a word or two with his favourite Alva, of whom there's no end of talk when he begins. He is so taken by her cooking skills and sense of colour and line combinations when picking seasonal dresses.'

'Oh yes, she is rather fussy about dresses.'

'There is, perhaps, a hidden artist in her that finds expression in her exquisite sense of colours and lines when she chooses dress materials or dresses for herself or for the purposes of gifts.' Vidya remarked in appreciation of her choices. 'I'm sure such aesthetic sense must reflect even in her setting up of the home with curtains and cushions.'

The day was fast advancing close to lunchtime, and there was still no trace of Vikram.

Meanwhile, Vidya quietly spoke up. 'You know I always wanted to be a nurse. But it never happened. I never got the chance to pursue my dream.'

There was a moment of silence as Ruby and Premchand absorbed Vidya's words. Then Ruby spoke up. 'You know what, Vidya? It's never too late. You can still become a nurse if that's what you really want.'

Vidya shook her head sadly. 'It's too late now.'

Premchand chimed in. 'And we can all chip in and help you out.'

Vidya's eyes filled with tears as she looked at both of them. 'Thank you,' she said. 'That means so much to me.'

Premchand further added to the effect by walking in a mock strut across the end of the room. He acted out Ruby's role, the crook of his left arm holding an imaginary clipboard as he pretended to write with his right hand. They burst out in laughter, enjoying the jovial moment. Ruby was glad and felt buoyant to have been received in her new environment without any glitches.

And with that, the women bonded even more deeply, united in their support of Vidya's unfulfilled dream and their commitment to helping her make it a reality.

The party had to break up because Ruby indicated she had better have her wash and get ready before the people from Subathu arrived. She collected her toilet bag and made a beeline to the bathroom.

In fact she was still perched on the little cushioned stool in front of the dressing table in an aura of fragrances, trying to look presentable to Vikram. Although, by now, she had outgrown her adolescent general fascination for appearances. Indeed she had grown into admiring Vikram for much more than common accomplishments, hailed so much by the mundane commonalty. It was rare, she thought, to find easily a person of such abiding allegiance to the age-old values that have stood the test of general ravages of time. They called him a reliable friend, one who gave a helping hand in the time of a fall, one who stood by his commitments, though going by his appearance, he was gruff and stern. He seemed to have long understood that truth is not always pleasant to the ears unless spoken by a poet or a glozing, smiling villain.

From the entrance at the main road to the Rana house was just about three minutes of a winding climb. For the oldies, perhaps, it would take twice as much time. Divya almost always took less than three minutes. She just went leaping and scampering up. For one thing, she always seemed to be in a hurry to reach the top. Her visits weren't frequent and long, and she invariably cut short on the climbing time. And though she reached home half out of breath, she made it a quick step indeed. Just midway, she began to shout for

Mastram to come down to the wicket gate to carry Daddy's bags and water bottle while he took his time climbing up the path. He not only enjoyed the beauty of the flower beds and the overhang of the cedars and a few pines but gave his sharp searching look around to make his mind up on how things were going on in the maintenance of the estate. He didn't have any doubts about Vidya's ability to get things done meticulously as per the standards. He took his leisurely time climbing and breathing the clean air.

In contrast, Divya was already in the living room and sharing a quick hug and kiss with her mom. She stood, for a moment, speechless by the window, and with a single look at Ruby, she recognized her from the description of hers her father had given and an old picture he had shown her. And then she leapt with a long stride and open arms to embrace Ruby and kiss her. Ruby responded likewise and saw that young Divya's eyes were misty. She was half laughing and half trying to overcome her oncoming emotional convulsions. Indeed, they all had a few minutes to settle down just as Vikram appeared at the door. Smiling at Vidya, he strode towards Ruby and took her in his arms for just a moment too long, kissed her, and withdrew to take another look at her. And from the approval in his eyes, he led her to another chair around the table and sat down beside her. The unimaginable proximity with Ruby sparked a rare feeling in him. It naturally followed a long and circuitous conversation between the two about Ruby's family and other related matters; the others watched in pleasant amazement. All of them, especially Vidya, were glad to notice that it didn't take Vikram long to regain his poise and be his natural self with his normal demeanour. He shifted his attention to Vidya as he seemed to have caught himself too long engaged in a tête-à-tête with Ruby while ignoring the others. He went up to his wife, hugged and kissed her, then led her into the chair she evidently was seated in before he came in.

There was still time before lunch, perhaps taken a bit later than usual today. Indeed, there was hustle and movement in the kitchen. Mastram shot out from a side door and began laying the table in the dining room across the corridor. He had changed into a smarter outfit with a starched turban. Vikram had once taken him out to his bungalow in Subathu for a couple of weeks to learn proper serving etiquette at the table. By his grooming and temperament, Vikram was a man of discipline, good aesthetic taste and style, and his oft-repeated declaration was, 'I'm a methodical man. Little mundane things get easily done and in quick time. One is left with a lot more time and peace of mind to devote to matters one may decide to and when.'

'You know, Ruby, Divya has been a hosteller for the last ten years, so I think she would soon be good friends with you once she decides. Her matron of the hostel told me at the parent–teacher meeting that not only does she excel in her academics as in her athletics but she is also good at socializing. She makes lots of friends by means of her gift of the gab. But at the same time, she knows how to give everyone the slip and disappear into the recesses of the school library close to examinations when she is preparing and wants no distraction. Warm and affectionate at heart, I'm sure she'd win you over as her friend once she makes up her mind. I've told her stories about your devotion and work for your patients. How you have sessions of storytelling and how you sing devotional songs outside the wards in the sun to lift their spirits and prepare for life while they convalesce.'

It was a great surprise to Vikram when Ruby said, 'Oh don't you worry, she has already taken her first steps. Perhaps quite like a child, she gazed at me for a long moment when she first saw me, and then she clung to me like my own child. I'm sure we'll get along mighty well. And indeed, I'm really gladdened to know how accomplished she is. She's been reared well in the happy ambience of this home. For the present, though, we mustn't stand between her and her ambitious plans of eminence in the medical profession by specialising in cancer research at Oxford. I believe she has the beans to pursue and attain her ambition, especially with those certificates of proficiency in studies she has obtained already—Vidya just shared how well she is doing in her studies. And that she is the darling of her brothers, especially Vidyadhar, the middle one; he dotes on her, I'm told.'

'Yes, all three of them adore her. They eagerly wait for the festivals that celebrate the sibling bonds, raksha bandhan and bhai dooj, when she is here in Solan, and amid festivities, they have a brief holiday and come to stay with me in Subathu and enjoy horse rides and picnics there. Omdutt and Vidyadhar will be back from Simla sometime after five. They might be a little early today. Vidya has told them about your arrival. I'm sure they'd come home unless there is an emergency. Maybe we shall have our evening tea together. And if Vidyadhar can be counted upon, they may pick up some fresh patties from Spencer's. There's the dependable old faithful Sood's ABC, ready to deliver what you may choose to go with your tea. Aromatic vapours from the kitchen have fired my appetite, and if you all are ready, we can just go across into the dining room.' Vikram said, looking at Ruby with a reassuring smile.

'I thought you might like a lemon drink before you eat. We had coffee. I was waiting for you to say if you'd care for a cold drink.

'Any ordinary leisurely lunch, and I'd have asked for a gin and lime juice cordial. But I think with our journey from Subathu, we've already kept you waiting long enough. Let's eat. I'm sure Ruby, after this aperitif of such a loving welcome from this new-found family, your appetite has been amply whetted and nothing would be more welcome than fresh home-cooked food. Sita is by no means a trained cook, but the husband and wife take proper care of the cooking required by the family. Yet what is especially commendable is the fish curry she makes to go with rice. It makes those at the table lick their fingers.'

The sound of chairs being dragged across the carpeted floor filled the air as the group rose to their feet. They made their way to the dining room, taking their designated seats around the large oval table. Divya, in a rush to secure her spot, quickly sat down on one side of Ruby, while Vidya took the seat on the other side. This left Vikram with the remaining seat beside Vidya. Premchand, with a quick

half-wink directed towards his father, took the empty seat on the other side of the table. As they settled into their places, the clinking of silverware and the soft murmur of conversation filled the room.